I.S. 61 Library

DINOTOPIA
CHOMPER

by Donald F. Glut

Random House 🏠 New York

To my paleo-pals,
Ricardo Delgado and Pete Von Sholly.
Thanks for all the wonderful lunches,
during which we were all "chompers."

DINOTOPIA®

CHOMPER

Windy Point

Crystal Caverns

The Hatchery

Baz

Pooktook

Volcaneum

Polongo River

Cornucopia
Treetown

Deep Lake
Bent Root

Temple Ruins

NORTHERN PLAINS

CRACKSHELL POINT

BACKBONE MOUNTAINS

Rocky Pass

Prosperine

Sapphire Bay

Poseidos
(sunken)

RAINY
BASIN

Hadro
Swamp

Waterfall City

GREAT CANAL

SKY GALLEY CAVES

Amu River

Warmwater
Bay

Culebra

OUTER ISLAND

Sculpted Cliffs

Tentpole of the Sky

Sky City

Thermala

The Time Towers

Canyon City

Ancient Gorge

Red Rapid
Canyon

Pteros

The Sentinels

FORBIDDEN MOUNTAINS

GREAT DESERT

The Portal

Sauropolis

Dolphin Bay

Dragonfly Coast

BLACKWOOD
FLATS

Chandara

Cape Turtletail

CHAPTER 1

Perry Taylor finished lowering the drawbridge. "Finally!" he said.

It was still morning. The young man walked up beside Stoutpoint, the short-horned dinosaur that had accompanied him to this familiar spot, and patted the saurian's smooth snout. Before them stood an ancient vertebral drawbridge, stretching forward like the bones in a sauropod's neck. On the other side of the bridge, as far as Perry could see, was thick forest.

"Are you *sure* you want to do this?" Stoutpoint squawked.

Perry smiled. Stoutpoint had been Perry's friend for many years. As a Montanoceratops, he was bigger than any of the Protoceratops individuals Perry had seen on his infrequent visits to Waterfall City and Sauropolis. And yet Stoutpoint would never approach the size of the largest horned dinosaurs, like Torosauruses and Triceratops.

"I appreciate your concern," Perry said. "But I

never break a promise. Besides, I'm not a hatchling anymore."

Actually, Perry wasn't as confident as he was trying to sound. This was, after all, the Rainy Basin he was looking at, home to Dinotopia's carnivorous dinosaurs. Many of them were fierce, unpredictable creatures that had long ago chosen to reject civilization and continue living according to the "old ways." He recalled "Honest" John Matthews, back in the village, and the tales the old merchant had often told about this place. For a moment, Perry felt an unsettling tingle run up and down his spine.

"B-but…" Stoutpoint was plainly fishing for the right words. "No one—human or saurian—ever goes there *alone*…at least, not if they plan on coming back."

Perry knew that perfectly well. But a certain big theropod was, after all, the very reason Perry had come here. The reason that, after so many years, he had journeyed back to the Rainy Basin.

"If you've *got* to go," the Montanoceratops went on, "at least let me go with you. Like last time—for protection."

"As I recall, last time turned out somewhat differently than you expected." Perry shook his head. "Thanks, but not this time. Anyway, I have my own protection."

Perry fingered the Giganotosaurus tooth that always hung from a thong around his neck. It was milky white in color and about six inches long. The tip was sharp and the edge jagged. For a moment, the tooth caught the sunlight and glowed brightly.

Stoutpoint snorted. "You really believe that old tooth will save you if some tyrannosaur decides to make you his dinner?"

"I'll be fine," Perry said, trying hard to believe his own words.

Stoutpoint was grumbling. "Easy for you to say," he said. "Do I need to remind you what short memories some of those big meat-mongers have? It's been so long!"

"Has it really?" Perry asked.

"Ten years," Stoutpoint said. "Which isn't long enough for me." The saurian shook his head, the end of which widened into a frill. "Well, if you insist on going alone, I'm not going to budge from this spot until you've returned safely. Even if it takes forever!"

"I'll be back in less time than that, I promise," Perry said. "And it won't be as some carnivore's main course."

Stoutpoint snorted.

"He'll remember me," said Perry. "I know he will."

"You *hope* he will," the saurian replied.

Perry sighed. "Breathe deep, seek peace," he said. With a last wave, he started across the bridge.

The young man had been walking for a while, first

along the Cross Basin Trail and then through thick forest. He was trekking now beneath a great canopy of trees that blocked out much of the sunlight. The ground, dense with vegetation, was still wet with dew.

Although ten years had gone by, much of the Rainy Basin was as Perry remembered it. Only the flora had changed. The main trails—long stretches of barren ground bearing the footprints of countless theropods—were still there. Other landmarks, including a large, pyramid-shaped rock and the remnants of an ancient meteorite, pointed the way to Perry's destination. Trees cluttered what the boy had remembered as open areas, while a large clearing he recalled from before was now home to a family of cycads.

If this had been any other day, Perry would have delighted in the variety of plant life around him. He would have noted the ferns and the trees and even the weeds he knew by name, and paid special attention to those plants that were new to him. Today, however, he had other things on his mind. Every sound, every movement, every stirring of the underbrush captured his attention. The Rainy Basin was a treacherous place, and his survival depended on his staying alert and watchful.

So far, Perry had not encountered any real danger. At one point, he'd hidden behind the thick trunk of a conifer tree as a fin-backed reptile crawled by. Dimetrodon, Perry thought as the lizardlike animal disappeared into the foliage.

Except for the Dimetrodon and a few lizards, Perry hadn't seen any animals since leaving Stoutpoint on the bridge. It was almost as if the Rainy Basin had prepared for his arrival, clearing the way for him with a green carpet of vegetation.

Perry touched the tooth hanging from his neck. Was it possible that it possessed some magical, protective power? Perry grinned. He'd like to think so, but when it came right down to it, he didn't believe it. More likely, his scent and the sound of his footsteps had been carried through the basin with the cool morning breeze. Besides, his return shouldn't be a surprise. Hadn't he and the one he sought agreed to meet on this very day, the anniversary of the first day of their adventure?

Finally, Perry reached his destination, a clearing about the size of his own village square. This was one of those rare spots in the Rainy Basin where the sunlight succeeded in reaching the ground. Breathing deeply, Perry settled down to wait, but he did not have to wait long. Almost immediately he heard the *thump, thump, thump* of approaching theropod footsteps.

The young man's body tensed. Had he grown enough to face whatever was about to make its entrance? Or would it be like it was so many years ago, when the mere presence of something new…something threatening…was enough to make him feel so…?

Perry looked up as the trees at the edge of the clearing parted to reveal the approaching giants. There were three of them, each at least forty feet long. Superficially, they somewhat resembled the great Tyrannosaurus rex. But these animals were stockier in build, and they boasted three large fingers on each hand rather than the tyrannosaur's diminutive two.

Giganotosaurs!

Perry had come to the right place.

The titans stood in a row at the edge of the clearing. Their slate-gray, yellow, and green hides shone brilliantly in the sunlight. All three animals were adults; two were male, one was female.

The dinosaurs sniffed, tipping their scaly heads down toward the young human.

Perry tried to control his fear. Any one of these magnificent animals could make a meal of him in seconds. What if these theropods were members of a different tribe? Or what if they were the right theropods, but had forgotten…or no longer cared?

The Giganotosaurus in the middle cocked his head. Though he was the younger of the two males, he was longer by several feet and the more powerfully built. Perry noted the distinctive patterns on his leathery hide. Yes, the animal was much, much bigger now, but still…it was *him!*

Perry held up the tooth for all three dinosaurs to see. It was identical to the many lining their own huge jaws. The larger male leaned forward, bringing his bumpy snout to within inches of Perry's face. The Giganotosaurus's eyes were focused directly on Perry's. His lips were pulled back slightly, revealing an impressive row of teeth.

Perry reached out, his fingers only inches away from the dinosaur's scaly snout. And he remembered twelve long years ago, when the Giganotosaurus tooth he now wore around his neck was not so much as a dream…

CHAPTER 2

It had been almost a week since an earthquake had rocked the area around the Polongo River. Located several miles to the southeast, the small village of Greenglen was again a quiet place. A craggy-faced merchant walked across the main street to his vendor's stand. With a quick yank of his powerful left arm, he drew away a cotton canopy to reveal the tools and other hardware he was offering for trade.

The old man looked around. Already people and saurians were in the street. Two villagers at a nearby stall were bartering for a cloak that was just the right size for their Plateosaurus friend. A plate-backed Kentrosaurus and three human friends were sharing a bucket of fruit juice. At the far end of the street, a half dozen boys and girls were riding dinosaur mounts toward the village park.

"Good morning, Mr. Matthews!"

A brown-haired boy was pushing a wheelbarrow across the street. In the wheelbarrow was a basket filled with ripe tomatoes.

"You're ten minutes late," grumbled the man.

Perry Taylor did not relish having to visit Honest John Matthews, even when it was just to complete a trade for his mother. The man always seemed to be in a bad mood, and this morning was no exception. Maybe Mr. Matthews didn't like children, Perry thought. But the merchant showed the same attitude toward grownups, too. It was as if Mr. Matthews held everyone in Greenglen responsible for the arm he had lost so many years ago.

"I'm...I'm sorry, Mr. Matthews," Perry apologized. "I...guess I overslept."

"And not the first time, either. Hmmphf!" Mr. Matthews grunted. He eyed the basket of tomatoes. "There's a whole gross here?"

Perry nodded. "Counted them myself," said the boy.

"I'll count 'em *myself* later. And the new garden tools're working out okay?"

"Mother likes them just fine," answered Perry.

"Knew she would," said Mr. Matthews. "My wares're always top-notch." The merchant stepped up to the wheelbarrow and tried to grasp the basket of tomatoes with his one arm.

Perry hesitated. He was never sure of what to say around adults, and around Mr. Matthews in particular. Now, as had happened so many times before, he was getting that strange feeling that held him back from doing what he wanted to do or knew he should do. Finally, he reached out toward the basket. "Here," he said, "let me help."

Mr. Matthews glared at him. "Never mind," he said. "I'm not helpless, you know." With renewed effort, the merchant braced the basket against his chest and hoisted it out of the wheelbarrow. Then he set it on the counter of his vendor's stand.

"Well," said Perry, feeling uncomfortable. He felt a little rumble in his stomach. "Mother's making breakfast. See you later, I guess."

Mr. Matthews complained under his breath as Perry rushed away down the street.

"All right, Perry," his mom called to him from the kitchen. "Breakfast's ready."

"One more minute," the boy called back to her.

Perry stood in his bedroom amid what his mother called "clutter," but which Perry regarded as priceless. By now, there were too many items in his collection to count. They seemed to fill every available space in the small bedroom, although the boy could always make room for one or two more. There were rock and soil samples of all kinds, pieces of tree bark, palm fronds, pressed leaves, and the skeletons of small animals and the exoskeletons of insects. Each item had been collected by Perry himself. Each was adorned with a descriptive label, neatly written in Perry's own hand, identifying the item and its place of origin.

Almost as important as the items themselves were

the memories they triggered of past exploratory adventures. The boy had not been on such an adventure since the earthquake. Already he was yearning to set out again and add some other piece of natural history to his little home museum.

In one corner of the room, piled into a pyramid-like shape, were the numerous scrolls he'd borrowed from the tiny village library—scrolls about nature, the habits of saurians, Dinotopian geology and history— whatever caught his interest.

Perry and his mother, Agnes, had lived in this house for seven years now, almost since the day they'd arrived on Dinotopia's shores. His memories of his life before they came here were vague—except for that one fateful night. Perry had been just six years old when the unexpected storm had struck his parents' boat. He could still feel his mother's arms as she swam with him to the safety of land. And he could still see his father making a final effort to save their boat…

Now thirteen years old, Perry knew he would never forget.

Perry shook his head. No sense dwelling on the past, he thought. He turned his attention to the creature occupying one of several small boxes that were covered by wire mesh. Like other animals he had taken in, this creature—a small winged lizard that Perry had identified as an Icarosaurus—had been injured. The small tear in one of the lizard's wings—both of which were now folded back along the sides of the animal's body—had healed nicely.

Perry removed some pieces of spinach from a small jar and hand-fed them to the lizard. The little reptile devoured them greedily, then began shaking his head from side to side.

"Perry!" his mother called again.

"I'm coming!" he answered, feeding the last of the spinach to his winged friend. He replaced the mesh covering.

"Don't you think it's about time to let him go?"

Perry turned to see his mother standing in the doorway.

In truth, Perry had grown fond of the lizard, feeding and nurturing it every day for the past few weeks. But what his mother said was true. The animal's injury had healed, and there was no longer any reason to keep it confined.

Nodding to his mother, Perry carried the box to an open window and pulled off the wire mesh. The Icarosaurus looked this way and that, then slowly unfolded its wings. Spread to their full length, the colorful wings reflected the morning sunlight. The lizard needed no coaxing; it sprang from the box and out the window, gliding through the air like a kite. Within moments, the animal was gone.

Perry felt a hand on his shoulder and looked up to see his mother's smiling face.

Perry sat in the small kitchen eating his second helping of the breakfast of berries and nuts his mother had prepared for him. As he ate, he occasionally glanced out the open window.

Something was happening in Greenglen today—something that happened in the village every year around this time. Perry could hear the distant sounds of children laughing and cheering.

"I think you've had enough blueberries," his mother said. "I don't want you to get an upset stomach."

"You're right," Perry said. Just one berry more, he thought, and he might burst. "I'll give Stoutpoint the rest."

"Well, at least we know they won't go to waste," Perry's mother said. She looked toward the open window, reacting to the cheery voices outside. "I guess it's that time of year again," she said.

"Guess so," said Perry quickly. "Well, see you later." He pushed himself up from the round breakfast table, which had been carved to resemble the Round Table in Waterfall City.

"Going to join the other children?" she asked.

"I don't know," he said, scooping the remaining blueberries into a small container. He could hear his mother's quiet sigh as he left the house.

"They're really very nice, you know," she said, her voice trailing after him.

Perry knew that his mother meant well. She frequently suggested that he get more involved in activities with other children his age. But he was interested in so many things that they were not…

Besides, Perry thought, did he really need any other friends when he already had Stoutpoint?

Perry stepped outside to see the Montanoceratops—who had grown too large to squeeze through the kitchen door—basking in the warm sunlight. The young dinosaur's horns and frill were noticeably larger than they had been a year ago. In another year, Stoutpoint would look very much like the adults in his family group.

"How are your mother and father?" Perry asked.

"Stout and hardy as always," replied the ceratopsian. Noticing the treat in Perry's hand, he immediately perked up. "Hmmm? For me…?"

"As if you didn't know," said Perry, holding the berries out toward Stoutpoint's beaked mouth. The boy enjoyed watching Stoutpoint eat almost as much as the animal enjoyed eating.

"Guess we should go and watch, at least," said Perry.

"Watch what?" asked Stoutpoint.

Perry turned his head in the direction from which the sounds of children were coming.

Swallowing a mouthful of blueberries at once, Stoutpoint nodded in agreement. The two of them headed toward the park at the end of Greenglen's main road.

* * *

The park was actually just a large open area that the villagers used for gatherings like picnics and fairs. Today it was a practice field for sports involving humans and saurians.

A group of some twenty village boys and girls—some about Perry's age, others slightly older—were busy practicing for the Dinosaur Olympics, which were held each year in the settlement of Cornucopia. Ring Riding, Racing, Tests of Strength—these and all the other sports were in evidence as the young riders put their willing dinosaurian steeds through their paces.

One of the riders, a tall, blond-haired boy named Elias, who was just two years older than Perry, was practicing his standing mount on the back of a running Gallimimus named Sleekneck. Elias gave Perry and Stoutpoint a friendly wave.

"Hey, Perry!" shouted Elias as he passed by. "Come and join us!"

Perry waved back as the other boy artfully guided his graceful, ostrichlike mount across the dusty ground. "Elias is going to do well in Ring Riding again this year," Perry said. "But then he always does. His dad used to be a real champ, you know."

Stoutpoint nodded. The horned dinosaur turned toward his friend. "Perry, are we going to enter this year?" he asked. "There are events just made for a young and healthy Montanoceratops."

Perry watched Elias for a few more moments. The

older boy had total confidence in himself and what he was doing. For a few moments, Perry thought about running up to the group and joining them. But he had that feeling again, not unlike the one he'd experienced earlier that day with Mr. Matthews. Something seemed to be holding him back.

He wasn't interested in sports anyway, Perry told himself.

"Let's go, Stoutpoint," he said. "It's been a while since we had ourselves a real adventure."

"Whatever you want to do, I'm with you," replied the Montanoceratops.

Walking side by side, Perry and Stoutpoint left the field behind them.

Perry led Stoutpoint back to the house and hitched him to the family wagon. The lad climbed aboard, taking his place in the driver's seat, just in front of the canvas top.

Stoutpoint glanced back at Perry. "North road?" he asked.

Perry nodded.

And so, with Stoutpoint pulling and Perry in the driver's seat, the rickety wagon was soon rolling out of the village. As with so many of their previous expeditions, Stoutpoint and Perry had no real notion as to where they were headed. Of one thing, however, Perry was certain: The more distance he and Stoutpoint put between himself and that practice field, the better.

CHAPTER 3

Neither Perry nor Stoutpoint had been paying much attention to where they were going. Perry had been too busy studying the plants, insects, animals, and rock formations they passed. Occasionally, they had to stop and maneuver around a fissure left by the earthquake.

Eventually, they came to a forest. Some of the thick-trunked trees—Taxodium, Perry thought—had been toppled over. Probably from the earthquake, guessed Perry. From a nearby pond emerged what at first appeared to be a snake. When it was entirely out of the water, Perry and Stoutpoint could see that it was a twenty-foot-long lizard with an extremely long neck. Clutched in its toothy jaws was a small armored fish.

"I've never seen anything like that before," said Stoutpoint.

"Tanystropheus," Perry said. "Lucky for us he eats only marine animals and insects."

They watched as the reptile gulped down his fishy

prize. Clumsily, the animal slipped into an earth fissure, then, still eating, quickly climbed out again and continued on his way.

Perry continued to comment on the fauna and flora until Stoutpoint changed the topic. "You know," the dinosaur said, "I'm in the best shape I've ever been in. Maybe I can't gallop or sprint like Sleekneck. But when Race Day rolls around, I can certainly beat any ol' Triceratops or Chasmosaurus."

Perry replied with a low "Hmmm…"

"Not only that," Stoutpoint continued, "but I'm pretty strong for a dinosaur of my size. In fact, when it comes to those Tests of Strength…"

The boy shook his head, his brown eyes focused on the rugged terrain passing by. "I'm sorry," said Perry. "But I'm *not* entering the Dinosaur Olympics. I'm just, well…you know, I'm not good at those kinds of things."

"How do you know?" Stoutpoint asked. "Maybe you'd be great. Maybe the two of us would make a great team, if we made an effort."

"It's just that…" Imagining it, Perry got that feeling he experienced whenever he had to assert himself or be aggressive or confrontational. And he didn't like it. "Well, it may be fun for you, but it definitely isn't for me."

"You don't have to win, you know," the dinosaur reminded him. "Remember, winning isn't the only reason for the Dinosaur Olympics. There's fair play, and the feeling of competition, and—"

"I know, I know," Perry interrupted. "But with kids like Elias, it hardly seems worth the effort. Maybe if I'd had a dad like his to…"

For a moment, Perry remembered that night on the water.

"Elias's father only helps him," Stoutpoint was saying. "It is Elias himself and his determination to succeed that—"

"But Elias is *interested* in the things he does," said Perry. "He loves doing them, and that's why he's so good. Me, I'd rather find a plant or rock that I've never seen before. Come on, we're supposed to be explorers. So let's do some exploring."

Stoutpoint sighed. "All right," he said. "By the way, fellow explorer…" Stoutpoint brought the wagon to a stop and looked around. "Do you have any idea where we are? I hope we're not in the horsetails."

Perry could identify most of the nearby plants by name, and the insects within view were all familiar, too. But other than that, nothing looked familiar.

Good! Perry thought. Unexplored territory!

Still continuing northward, Perry and Stoutpoint came at last to a trail that had been pounded out over many years by the stomping feet of countless dinosaurs.

"Well, we know one thing for sure," commented

"...trail's got to lead *somewhere*." He *Stoutpoint* brought his beaked nose close to the trail and sniffed. Suddenly, he snorted and backed up. "Theropods!" he said.

Perry was shocked. What were theropods doing on this side of the river? How had they gotten over here? "We'd better check it out," he said.

Stoutpoint swung his head around. "Are you sure that's a good idea?" he asked.

"Like I said, we're explorers," said Perry, trying his best to sound brave. "And we've come this far. A little farther won't hurt."

For a moment, Perry thought Stoutpoint was going to turn around anyway. "Okay, but just a little farther," he finally said.

Theropods! Perry thought. He was scared, but also excited. He'd read about them but never actually seen any. He wondered if they'd be as impressive as he'd always imagined.

Continuing onward, they saw in the distance something neither of them had ever seen before, but which they'd often heard described by the adults in their village. Now, only several hundred feet away was the great expanse of bridge that connected their region to the Rainy Basin.

The bridge was magnificent to behold. According to a scroll Perry had read, it had been built long ago by some of Dinotopia's original human and saurian residents. It stretched for some four hundred feet, maybe more, across the deep gorge and the trailing Polongo River below.

As they drew closer, Perry was surprised to see that the drawbridge had been lowered.

"So that's how those theropods got over here," Perry said. "It must have been knocked down by the earthquake. Remind me to tell Mother and the elders when we get home."

Stoutpoint stopped. "I think this is far enough," he said.

For once, Perry had to agree. Although humans and most saurians had long lived together in harmony on the island, the meat-eating dinosaurs—especially the big ones, like the tyrannosaurs—could and usually did mean trouble for anyone bold or foolish enough to enter their domain.

The meat-eating dinosaurs, just like the plant-eaters, needed to survive. And survival meant utilizing the adaptations that were natural to them, including their sharp teeth and claws. The tyrannosaurs and their saurian cousins meant no malice toward their prey. They hunted and scavenged and fed in the only way they knew how and by the best means at their disposal.

Unfortunately, those meat-eating giants seemed to be hungry more often than not and were usually not too particular about where they got their meals.

"Don't forget what old man Matthews told us," said Stoutpoint.

Perry did not need to be reminded. Mr. Matthews often told the story about the spice caravan he'd led through the Rainy Basin and the hungry Allosaurus that had taken his right arm.

"Let's get away from here," Perry said, shivering. "I think there are some temple ruins not too far away. Let's go there."

The Montanoceratops started to turn the wagon. "As long as those ruins are farther away from the Rainy Basin—"

"Skrawww!"

"What was that?" Perry asked.

Stoutpoint had frozen in place. "I don't know," he said, "but I don't like it."

The sound reminded Perry of the chirping of a bird. But it was much deeper in pitch and many times louder than any bird.

The sound came again.

"Something is boiling in the pot," said Stoutpoint.

"Let's investigate," Perry said excitedly.

Before Stoutpoint could answer, Perry climbed down from the wagon.

"Perry!" Stoutpoint hissed.

"I'll be careful," Perry said.

"Skraaaww! Skrawww!"

Whatever it was, it seemed to be coming from somewhere up ahead. Perry followed the sound, the Montanoceratops keeping close behind him.

The short natural trail ended at a tear in the

ground—another remnant of the recent earthquake. The fissure measured some ten feet across and five feet deep. Not too deep for him to climb into nor, with a bit more effort, out of.

However, it was what was at the bottom of the fissure that instantly seized the boy's attention.

"Skraaaawwww…!"

The squawking creature was definitely a theropod, though a very small one. Its head and eyes looked too big for its body, and the hind limbs seemed overly long. It was still a hatchling, Perry realized. It belonged in a nest, tended by its parents.

As the theropod let out another *skrawww*, Perry could see that its teeth were tiny, barely hinting at the dangerous weapons they would someday become.

"A baby Tyrannosaurus?" asked Stoutpoint, poking his snout over Perry's shoulder.

Perry shook his head. "Look at his hands. This little fellow's got three fingers. With his looks and coloring, I'd say he's a Giganotosaurus."

"Giganotosaurus!" Stoutpoint said. "They grow even *bigger* than tyrannosaurs. Which means they've got bigger appetites. And bigger *parents*."

Stoutpoint looked around quickly, as though he expected the hatchling's parents to materialize out of thin air.

Perry was shaking his head. "I'm guessing that this little guy got separated from his mom and dad during the earthquake. Somehow he crossed the bridge and plopped down into this hole."

"I feel sorry for him," said Stoutpoint. "But I suggest we leave this place, and right away, in case his parents decide to come looking for him."

The Giganotosaurus hatchling continued to squawk, opening his mouth as wide as he could.

"If that were true," Perry said, "wouldn't they have found him by now? The poor thing's so hungry."

"H-hungry?" said Stoutpoint.

"I read that dinosaurs like this are kind of like birds. They can't live on their own until they're older and bigger. And they need their parents...to feed them."

"Feed?" Stoutpoint reacted with a start. "Perry, you can't mean—!"

Perry certainly did. When he was small and helpless, someone had saved his life. This was his chance to return the favor.

Looking around fast, Perry spotted some bushes. He yanked off two big handfuls of the foliage, and then cautiously eased his way down into the fissure.

The dinosaur's already distinct neck muscles tightened as the head drew back, jaws open. The little carnivore snapped at Perry, missing him by mere inches.

"Perry, get out of there!" Stoutpoint warned. "Remember Mr. Matthews. It'll bite your hand off!"

"I don't think so," said Perry. "I'm betting the little guy's so hungry, he'll eat anything..." Perry stepped back, his eyes locked on the hatchling's. "Especially if it's fed *to* him."

"Please be careful," Stoutpoint said softly.

And careful Perry was. As he moved closer, he extended a hand toward the animal's scaly snout.

"Skkkwarrrrr…?"

Perry waited until its open mouth jutted toward him again. And when it did, Perry quickly shoved in a handful of vegetation.

The hatchling clamped his jaws shut. He cocked his gray and yellow head and sniffed at the vegetation hanging from his mouth. Then he gulped down the meal of greens.

"You see!" exclaimed Perry. "He's so hungry, he'll eat anything!"

"Or anyone," grumbled Stoutpoint.

"No, look," said the boy, taking a step closer. Cautiously, he reached out and stroked the top of the animal's head, feeling the mosaic of smooth scales.

Stoutpoint shook his head. "I just hope he's heard the old saying about not biting the hand that feeds you."

"Skrraaaa…" This time the sound was low and mellow.

"You still hungry?" asked the boy. "Ready for a second helping?"

The Giganotosaurus cocked his head again, as if to answer.

Perry fed him the other handful of foliage, which the hatchling eagerly devoured.

"He's a real chomper, isn't he?" said Perry, watching the young saurian with delight.

"I'll say," sighed Stoutpoint. "He eats more than I do, and he's just a fraction of my size."

"He'll like blueberries even more."

"Blueberries? Where are we going to find blueberries around here?"

Perry grinned.

The horned dinosaur's eyes opened wide. "You're not thinking…"

"Give me a hand," said Perry. "Or, better yet, a snout."

"But, Perry, you don't know what you're doing."

"A snout, please?" Already the youth was placing his arms around the Giganotosaurus hatchling. The animal squirmed a bit, his oversized feet flailing about, but the little dinosaur was not really resisting.

"Oof! He's heavy!" Perry said.

Squawking a complaint, Stoutpoint leaned his head down into the fissure, careful not to slip off the edge. He shut his eyes as Perry hoisted the hatchling onto his snout.

The ceratopsian turned and set the theropod on the ground as Perry pulled himself out of the fissure. Before the hatchling had time to scamper away, Perry grasped him in his arms and pushed him through the opening of the wagon's canvas covering.

Stoutpoint looked disapprovingly at Perry.

"Look," said Perry, climbing back aboard the wagon, "we can't just leave the little fellow out here to starve, can we?"

"I…guess not," replied Stoutpoint. "But he's a theropod! What are you going to feed him? I don't think he's going to want to eat bushes for the rest of his life."

"I'll think of something," answered Perry.

"And what about when he gets bigger?"

"I've cared for orphaned animals before," said the boy, although this hatchling was hardly in the same league as the lizards, turtles, and birds he'd kept in the past. "Isn't that right, Chomper?"

The giganotosaur let out a loud *"Skkkrraaww!"*

"Chomper?" asked Stoutpoint, saying the name slowly.

"Have you got a better idea?"

"How about Trouble," said the horned dinosaur. "Because that's what this cute little guy is going to grow up to be. Fifty feet of nasty, hungry trouble."

"Come on, Stoutpoint," said Perry. "This expedition's over. Let's go home."

CHAPTER 4

It was just past noon when Stoutpoint turned down Greenglen's main street. Looking through the front opening of the wagon's canvas cover, Perry watched Chomper scampering excitedly about the wagon. So far, no one in the village had become aware of who or what the wagon harbored. But Perry was becoming increasingly worried about what would happen once they did.

"Skkkrawwwwk!"

Perry had given up trying to keep Chomper quiet. Actually, it hardly mattered. The wagon wheels were noisy enough to cover the hatchling's squawking.

Out of the corner of his eye, Perry could see the children practicing in the field. He would have loved to show off the hatchling to the other youths, especially Elias. But that would have to wait until later.

The people and dinosaurs of Greenglen were about their normal business, bartering, enjoying each other's company, or just taking in the noonday sun. Mr. Matthews was at his stand, discussing a trade with a young woman and a hadrosaur. The merchant's right side was facing the wagon, and Perry got a good look at the loose right sleeve of his jacket as the wagon rolled by.

"Hi, Mr. Matthews," said Perry, his voice cracking nervously.

For a moment, the merchant's frowning face glanced up.

Turning off the main street, Stoutpoint drew the wagon along several side roads. As they got closer to home, Perry tried to remember all the reasons why bringing back a baby theropod was a good idea.

Perry's mother was just finishing up her morning chores, hanging the last of the family's wet clothes on a line to dry. She looked up as they neared the house.

"The explorers return early from their expedition," she said. "But just in time for lunch."

"Remember," Stoutpoint said softly, "this wasn't my idea."

"Hi, Mom," said Perry.

"If you've brought something back," she said, "I hope it won't attract more dust."

"That's for sure," said Stoutpoint.

Perry suddenly found himself at a loss for words. Finally, he said, "He's in the wagon."

"He?" his mother replied, raising an eyebrow.

She stepped to the back of the wagon and looked through the canvas opening.

"Ssskkkrawwwwwkk!"

The wide-open mouth of the baby *Giganotosaurus* darted out at her, missing her face by inches. She fell back with a gasp.

"His name's Chomper," the boy said.

"I don't care what his name is!" Mrs. Taylor said, breathing heavily. "That's a…a Tyrannosaurus!"

The boy shook his head. "Giganotosaurus," he said. "Mom, I didn't know what to do. He was all alone and starving. I had to bring him back!"

"Giganotosaurus…Tyrannosaurus…" his mother said. "Either way, that little dinosaur will someday grow into a gigantic—and very dangerous—meat-eater!"

"I know, Mom," said Perry. "But I've been thinking. Maybe if he's brought up here, among people and civilized dinosaurs, and given a lot of love and attention…"

His mother was shaking her head. "No, it's impossible. You can't change a theropod's nature."

"But you once said," Perry started, "and the scrolls say, too, that the big meat-eaters live the way they do not because they have to but because they choose to. It's a choice. We can teach him to be civilized."

Perry's mom paused for a few moments, as if remembering something.

"You know, long ago, when I was a little girl in America," Perry's mother recalled, "a stray dog wandered up to our house. She was quite unfriendly, and my parents wanted to turn her away. Still, I fell in love with the dog. My dad finally let me take her in. But only if she was my responsibility and mine alone. And you know? After a while, she became the friendliest dog in the neighborhood."

"Chomper's already friendly," said Perry, extending a hand toward the hatchling. "See?"

"Perry—!" she said, trying to stop him.

But her son was already petting the top of the theropod's head and rubbing the underside of his lower jaw. Chomper's short, birdlike tongue vibrated up and down, and a quiet, contented rumbling issued from his throat.

Perry's mother shook her head in amazement. "Just for the sake of argument, what would you feed him?"

The boy rushed to the garden, returning moments later with two handfuls of blueberries. A moment later, one handful vanished down Chomper's throat.

"See, he likes plants!" said Perry.

"But maybe it's only because the first thing he ate was vegetation," said Stoutpoint. "What'll you feed him tomorrow if his natural craving for meat kicks in?"

Perry's mother nodded. "That's what I'm worried about."

"Maybe it won't," Perry rationalized. "I read somewhere that meat-eaters get vitamins and minerals that are found only in plants by eating plant-eaters. If Chomper eats plants, he's just skipping a step."

Stoutpoint looked up. "But don't meat-eaters need other things in their diet? Things that aren't found in plants?"

"You've taken in animals that needed help before," Perry's mother said, "but never anything like this."

Chomper, as if understanding, cocked his head and looked into Perry's mother's face.

She sighed. "Well…I've seen a lot of amazing things on this island. And you certainly know how to make a good argument. But we can't take on a responsibility as big as this without first getting the approval of the council elders."

"And while we're waiting for them to decide?" asked the lad.

"Remember," Agnes Taylor cautioned, "he's *your* responsibility."

Perry smiled and hugged the baby theropod as it gulped down the second handful of berries. "I'll make sure Chomper grows up as nice and friendly as your dog ever was."

"This I've got to see," commented Stoutpoint.

That afternoon, the residents of Greenglen saw something most of them would never have imagined: a thirteen-year-old boy, a Montanoceratops, and a Giganotosaurus cub walking down the main street together. The hatchling was hobbling on long, wobbly legs. His tail, held high off the ground, was wagging slightly from side to side. The little theropod pulled on his leash; Perry held the other end tightly.

Perry wasn't happy about his mother's firm suggestion that Chomper be leashed. Yet no one, to Perry's knowledge, had ever befriended a theropod like a giganotosaur before. And there was no telling what Chomper might do if left on his own. For now, at least, the leash seemed to be in the best interests of the baby Giganotosaurus as well as the people and saurians of Greenglen.

Within moments, a crowd of villagers had gathered in the street around Perry and his two friends.

"Kind of cuddly," stated an old man who was obviously keeping his distance from the hatchling.

"Everything is cuddly when young," replied an Iguanodon. "But in a year from now…?"

"Cave lion cubs are cute, too," said a woman. "But you know how they are when they're big…"

"Oh, but he's so small, so cute," a young woman said. She slowly reached out toward the hatchling. "I'd wager he's friendly, too, if he's Perry and Stoutpoint's friend." She extended her index finger toward Chomper's snout.

"Careful," said a man standing behind her. "You want to lose that finger?"

Chomper eyed the finger curiously. He tilted his head, stepped back and forth, then sniffed the woman's finger.

"Look at that," the young woman said. "He likes me. And I'll bet he'll like this, too." Rotating her hand around his head, she began to rub the Giganotosaurus under his chin.

Chomper made a gurgling noise that sounded to Perry almost like laughter.

"Tell me these ol' eyes are lyin' to me!"

Perry, Stoutpoint, and everyone else turned to see a red-faced Honest John storming toward them. The merchant stopped a few feet away from the hatchling and stared down at it with a look of disdain.

"For the life of me, it's a giganotosaur!" Mr. Matthews exclaimed. "And not much different from the one that took my arm. Right here in broad daylight on the main street of Greenglen!"

Perry was so nervous, he wished he could just disappear. He looked around at the rest of the villagers. No one would meet his eyes. It was up to him to defend Chomper. He turned to Honest John.

"But, Mr. Matthews," Perry said, "didn't you always tell us…I mean, wasn't it an adult Allosaurus that took your arm? Chomper's just a baby—"

"Allosaurus, Giganotosaurus, Ceratosaurus, Tyrannosaurus," Honest John said. "To me, they're all the same. All bad, all hungry, all worthless vermin that ought to be exterminated."

John Matthews looked around the gathering in the street. "I'll never forget," he said, "how that big allosaur came bounding out of the brush. Took me by surprise, he did! And he took my arm, too. One clean bite."

Perry shuddered as he always did when Mr. Matthews told his story. The crowd murmured.

"And I tell you no meat-eating dinosaur—not even a baby one—has got a place in this village. We've got to get rid of that thing, and we've got to do it now!"

People in the group started to argue, some siding with Honest John, others supporting Chomper.

Stoutpoint raised his voice. "Mrs. Taylor, Perry's mother, is going to address the elders tonight. It will be up to them if Chomper stays in Greenglen or not."

Mr. Matthews smiled, showing his discolored teeth. "Then it won't be long before we're rid of the little pest."

That said, the old man turned and marched back to his stand.

Perry looked at Stoutpoint worriedly. Mr. Matthews was on the council and had a lot of influence with the other elders.

Just then, Elias pushed through the crowd, a look of awe and respect on his face.

"Perry Taylor!" he said. "I can't believe it! Imagine riding him, when he's bigger, in the Dinosaur Olympics!"

The expected questions followed—most of them about what Chomper would eat and how fast he would grow. Perry relaxed his grip on the leash and responded to their questions. At first he was hesitant to speak, but as the questions continued, he gradually felt better and better about it. He was even starting to enjoy the attention!

As the villagers came closer, Chomper tensed up, reacting to the many hands and claws moving around him on all sides. His head darted from side to side, as if trying to find a better angle from which to view the towering creatures all around him.

Finally, Elias reached in and stroked the Giganotosaurus's head. Chomper gurgled and squawked; his wide mouth almost seemed to be smiling. Soon all the onlookers were captivated by the hatchling's charm.

Then, without the slightest warning, Chomper bolted, pulling the leash out of Perry's hand and disappearing into the crowd.

"Chomper!" yelled Perry.

"I was afraid something like this was going to happen," Stoutpoint said.

Moving away from one another, the villagers looked about the street, but Chomper was nowhere to be seen.

"Now what?" asked the Montanoceratops.

Suddenly, they heard a scream. Seconds later, Mrs. Roth, the village baker, was standing outside her shop, gasping for breath and pointing toward the shop's open front door. "There's a…a…"

"Chomper!" exclaimed Perry and Stoutpoint together.

They rushed toward the bakery, with Elias and the others in fast pursuit. Perry rushed past Mrs. Roth and into the shop. Even before he saw him, the boy recognized the chirping sound Chomper made when he was especially happy.

The little shop was filled with wonderful aromas—peaches, apples, blueberries, and more—all mingled with the smell of baking crust. It was plain to see that Chomper, with his keen sense of smell, had detected these strange and new aromas back in the street.

Perry found the hatchling perched in an open window of the shop's back room. It was one of the windows where Mrs. Roth set her freshly baked pies to cool off. On the windowsill was an empty pie tin. Smeared all over the dinosaur's jaws were telltale blueberry stains.

Chomper grinned at Perry, showing off his teeth, which were now an appetizing shade of blue.

"I think it's time to go home," said Perry, stepping up to the window.

"Uh, here," said Mrs. Roth, holding out a second blueberry pie. "In case he's still hungry."

"Thanks," said Perry, accepting the pie on Chomper's behalf. "I'll see that he gets it."

Chomper cocked his head and licked his chops. Then, he sprang into Perry's arms, knocking the boy and the pie to the floor. He started gobbling again.

Sighing, Mrs. Roth fetched Chomper a third blueberry pie.

***

Later that evening, Chomper took his first steps inside the Taylor home. The dinosaur looked around curiously, his head turning sharply at the slightest sound.

Chomper and Perry were alone in the house. Perry's mother was talking to the village elders about Chomper, and Stoutpoint had returned to his own family for the night.

"This is where you're going to live," said Perry. He had reattached the leash and was holding on to it tightly.

Chomper looked at Perry and cocked his head to the side, trying to understand. Like the other dinosaurs of Dinotopia, Perry knew, giganotosaurs and the rest of the theropods were smart. Theropods had their own language, spoken in deep and guttural tones. It was a tongue distinct from that of humans and the other saurians, and extremely difficult for non-theropods to voice. However, Chomper hadn't been exposed to it long enough to pick it up. Instead, Perry realized, Chomper would be listening to the human tongue and trying to learn that. But because of the shape of his mouth and tongue, Chomper would never be able to speak it.

"You know, Stoutpoint understands some theropod," Perry said, "even though it's hard for him to pronounce the words. Maybe he could teach you—and me—some of your language. We might all learn from each other."

Chomper chirped happily, as if understanding at

least some of what Perry was talking about. Suddenly, the theropod reacted to another chirping. It was higher-pitched than his own and emanating from outside. Turning his head furtively, the dinosaur spotted a small, tailless pterosaur perched on a tree limb just outside the kitchen window.

With a quick movement, Chomper lunged for the open door. This time, however, Perry was ready and didn't let go of the leash. The boy collided with the kitchen table, bringing himself and the little dinosaur to an abrupt halt.

Outside, the startled pterosaur flew off into the slowly darkening sky.

Chomper looked back at Perry.

"Look, Chomper," he said, placing his arms around the hatchling. "If you're going to be part of this family, you're going to have to behave. Think you can at least try?"

The Giganotosaurus seemed to react, but Perry could not be certain. Taking a chance, he slipped off Chomper's leash. The theropod took a few steps this way and that, but otherwise did not budge from where he stood.

"Good," said the boy, stroking the dinosaur under his chin. "Now, can you follow me?"

Perry walked toward his room. The lad turned to see Chomper standing where he had left him. "This way," Perry said. "It's all right, come on."

Chomper hesitated for a few more seconds. Then

slowly, his eyes seeming to fix upon everything inside the house, he ambled across the floor.

Perry sat down on his bed. The theropod looked around, his senses absorbing every detail of the room. One by one, he looked over the items in Perry's collection. He poked his snout, nostrils sniffing, into the empty pens that had housed orphaned or hurt animals.

"You seem to be interested in things," said Perry. "All right, then…" And so, for the next hour, the lad talked to Chomper about almost every item in his collection. Whether or not the hatchling understood what Perry was saying wasn't important. What was important was that Chomper willingly remained close to Perry for more than an hour.

By mid-evening, Perry had gotten around to the empty wire-mesh boxes. "This one was the temporary home of a gliding lizard," said Perry, holding out the container for Chomper to sniff. "But once I felt he could survive on his own, I had to let him go." Saying those words, Perry wondered if the time would eventually come when he would feel the same way about Chomper. He didn't want to think about that, and he suddenly realized he might never have to as he heard the front door of the house open and shut.

"Mom?" he called.

Perry's mother came and stood in his doorway. She looked tired. "Mr. Matthews has a lot of clout with the other elders," she told him. "But they could not turn their backs on an abandoned orphan, theropod or otherwise. So, Chomper can stay—*if* he doesn't cause any trouble and if he spends most of his time here—at home."

Perry shouted for joy and hugged his new friend, feeling the cool mosaic of tiny scales against his cheek.

Perry slept well and long that night. His sleep was interrupted only once as the theropod shifted from the floor to the bed itself, curling up at the boy's feet.

CHAPTER 5

Over the next week, Stoutpoint was over every day, teaching Chomper the basics of the theropods' language. Perry began to show Chomper how to play some very basic games—mostly running side by side across an unplowed field and tug-of-war. Perry and Chomper also liked to wrestle. During such matches, Chomper showed Perry how to move quickly, while Perry taught Chomper how to turn an opponent's strength against him. When the two were not playing, Perry was outside in the garden helping his mother with her chores.

His mother's new project was expanding the garden. Perry was using a wooden pole as a lever to remove rocks embedded in the soil. Chomper watched Perry as he worked, then set off prowling about the garden like some reptilian sabertooth cat, hunting for bugs.

The dinosaur had been insect-hunting every day now, scratching at the ground with his hind claws, sometimes leaning forward to rake at the dirt with his smaller front claws. Today, however, was the first time Perry actually saw Chomper snap up and devour one of the little creatures. Perry felt somewhat disturbed as he watched the hatchling unearth and then gobble up several more insects.

Stoutpoint walked up beside Perry. "Looks like his natural instincts are emerging."

"Oh, I don't know," Perry said. "I've been feeding him fruits and vegetables every day, and he still seems to like them. I'm hoping this bug-hunting may just be curiosity."

As he watched Chomper, Perry slowly realized that something seemed amiss. Chomper was moving sluggishly, and there was something different in the tone of his chirping. It was as if the theropod had lost some of his enthusiasm.

"Is something wrong with him?" Perry asked his horned-dinosaur friend.

"I think I know, but let's be sure."

As the twosome watched, Chomper sat down to rest. The dinosaur began to munch on some cabbages, but only halfheartedly. Clearly, something was wrong with the little fellow.

"What's wrong with him?" Perry asked. "Is he sick?"

"Chomper is a theropod," Stoutpoint said, "and theropods, just like the sabertooth cats, the big sea reptiles, and so many other kinds of animals, survive by eating other animals. Chomper may like the taste of blueberries, and they might indeed fill his belly. But berries, leaves, and cabbages can't nourish Chomper the way he needs to be nourished."

"What can we do?" Perry asked. "If he doesn't get nourishment, he'll die."

Then, suddenly, Perry had an idea.

The vast swamp near Greenglen was dark and gloomy, even in the daytime. It smelled of rotting vegetation and all kinds of animal life. No matter where one stepped, there would be something small and often unidentifiable skittering away underfoot.

Perry was flanked by the Montanoceratops on one side and the baby Giganotosaurus on the other. There was no clear trail or path; they pushed through tangled plants to forge ahead.

"At least this place is better than the Rainy Basin," said Stoutpoint as he maneuvered his way through the vegetation of the swamp, using his snout and beak to help clear a path.

"How do you know?" asked Perry with a chuckle. "Have you ever been there?"

The ceratopsian shook his head. "But I've heard enough about it."

Of the group, only Chomper seemed to enjoy their new surroundings. Frequently, he sniffed the air, enjoying the new smells the swamp offered. Again and again, he snapped at the flying insects buzzing all around him.

"Chomper doesn't seem to mind this place as much as we do," Perry observed. "I'll bet it's safer than the Rainy Basin, too. I've never heard of anything bigger than him actually living in this swamp."

"The local residents may be small, but as far as I'm concerned, size isn't everything when it comes to being unpleasant," Stoutpoint said, snapping his head to one side to avoid some mosquitoes.

Perry smiled. Already he could see where the narrow branch of a small river cut through a clearing beyond the trees.

A dragonfly, a Meganeura, with wings spanning more than two feet across, zipped overhead as Perry and his friends pressed onward. The clearing was brightly lit and could now be seen through the trees ahead.

"There," said Perry, patting Chomper's head. "Don't worry, little guy. You won't be hungry much longer."

Chomper let out a sad-sounding bleat as Perry led him toward the open space. The three friends stepped into the clearing, their feet squishing into the cool mud of the riverbank.

"Well," said Stoutpoint, looking around, "what's for lunch?"

Perry was already examining the soft ground at the edge of the water. He could see the multitude of insects—some of them tiny, others almost as big as Chomper himself—that crept and crawled and burrowed along or through the wet earth.

Chomper opened his mouth and flicked his tongue over his teeth. Then he cocked his head toward Perry, as if asking for permission to feed on the little creatures.

"Are you sure this is…right?" Perry asked the ceratopsian. The boy had been brought up as a vegetarian, as had all the people in his village. "I mean, maybe there's some other way."

Stoutpoint shook his head. "You're going to have to face the truth," the horned dinosaur said, his voice somber. "My parents explained it to me once. My kind—and most of the other saurians of Dinotopia that have followed the ways of civilization—are herbivores. To survive, we must eat plants and only plants. Theropods like Chomper are carnivores who must eat meat. There's no right or wrong about it. It's just nature's way. At least most of the big theropods have given up actually hunting down their prey."

"And what about me?"

"Humans are omnivores," Stoutpoint said. "They can live on plants or meat or both. But here in Dinotopia, humans have chosen to eat plants because so much of the animal life is intelligent. The animals Chomper can eat here, on the other hand, are not intelligent."

"But will Chomper really want to, er…*eat* those things?" the boy pondered, stepping away from a cluster of tiny spiders that had gathered around his right foot.

Chomper squawked.

"I think so," replied Stoutpoint. "But there's only one way to find out."

Taking a deep breath, Perry stooped down and gathered up a handful of hard-shelled things, whose rapidly moving appendages tickled his skin. Taking a closer look, he winced at the collection of Rochdalia cockroaches and other six-legged life-forms crawling across his open palm. Quickly, he held his hand out to Chomper. Cocking his head, the young theropod gingerly moved his snout nearer to the insects. Finally, he opened his jaws just enough for Perry to slip his hand—and the creepy delicacies—into his mouth, then out again.

"Yuck!" said Stoutpoint, looking away.

But Chomper chomped on the bugs, swallowed, then flicked his short tongue against his teeth and nodded affirmatively.

"I guess there's no accounting for taste," said Stoutpoint.

"There," said Perry, pointing to the muddy bank teeming with bugs, scorpions, and worms. "They're all, uh…for you."

Without any further hesitation, Chomper feasted. His snout and jaws plowed through invertebrates and mud alike. Again and again, the theropod did this until, at last, his stomach seemed to be satisfied.

"Whenever you're hungry, this is where we'll go," said Perry, stroking Chomper's back.

"At least for now," said Stoutpoint.

Chomper let out a happy and thankful *"Skkraaawwwkkk!"* and his tail swished stiffly from side to side. Then, he looked at Perry in a curious way, first eyeing the creeping and crawling things in the mud, then waving a three-fingered hand toward the boy's mouth.

"Er, I think he's asking you to join him for lunch," laughed Stoutpoint.

"Uh, thanks," said Perry, "but I've already had mine." The boy scanned the swamp. It was filled with a vast number and variety of creatures. "I don't think this swamp'll ever run out of food for you."

"Maybe not," interjected the Montanoceratops. "But those little bugs aren't going to keep your friend satisfied forever. His size is going to increase…and his taste and needs and appetite along with it."

Perry knew that Stoutpoint was right. For now, the relatively small insects and arthropods of the swamp would provide the nourishment Chomper needed to be healthy and grow. But someday, he'd require more substantial food if he ever hoped to grow into a powerful adult Giganotosaurus.

Feeding Chomper soon became Perry's main occupation. Scrolls in the village library offered some information regarding the feeding habits of meat-eating dinosaurs. These helped Perry decide what to do as his carnivorous friend got bigger…and hungrier.

Stoutpoint continued to be around much of the time, doing his best to teach the young carnivore the languages of both theropods and humans.

"*Rrreeaaarrgg!*" Perry growled, the low-pitched word putting a strain on his throat. "How was that?" he asked.

Chomper looked at the boy and tilted his head.

"If that was supposed to mean 'up,'" said Stoutpoint, chuckling, "you need a lot more practice."

Perry rubbed his throat. "I guess humans weren't designed to speak theropod," he said. "But that doesn't mean I won't stop trying."

In reply, Chomper made a noise that vaguely sounded like the word "good."

"My suggestion is that both of you stick mostly to your own languages," said Stoutpoint, "and leave the translating to me."

A month later, Perry, Chomper, and Stoutpoint were at the swamp again, making their regular visit to the riverbank.

"He's growing fast," said Perry to the ceratopsian. "Much faster than I am."

The boy looked over at the theropod walking beside him. Chomper was no longer a hatchling, but what the science scrolls would call a "juvenile." Indeed, the little fellow had about doubled in size since their first venture into this swamp. By now, his head was almost as high as Perry's.

Chomper had become accustomed to the river itself and seemed to enjoy wading into the shallow part, sometimes going in knee deep. On this day, Perry rolled up his trouser legs and joined his friend.

"Be careful," warned Stoutpoint from the bank. "There could be anything swimming or crawling in there."

Perry laughed. "Stoutpoint, sometimes you worry too much."

Even though the water was dark, Perry could see some of the denizens of the river. A small number of these creatures Perry knew by name. Countless tadpole shrimp called Tripos, identified by their long, segmented bodies, kept close to the river bottom. Tiny crawling creatures—he thought they were named Triassocoris—also stayed at the bottom, utilizing their very long, beaklike snouts in their own search for food. Numerous Palaegas, with their shield-shaped heads and segmented bodies, were busy swimming and scavenging for food. And there were much bigger and quite ugly creatures—were they called Halicyne? Perry thought—equipped with shield-like heads, stalked eyes, and five pairs of bristly legs.

Chomper seemed to enjoy the big jellyfish—Progonionemus, Perry thought they were called. Some of these sported tentacles almost as long as their bodies were wide. Chomper also relished the many varieties of giant worms and ancient crayfish, chomping them down before Perry had time to identify them.

Day after day, Chomper dined there. But after just a couple of weeks, Perry began to notice something disturbing. The theropod was eating with less enthusiasm. Finally, one afternoon, the dinosaur simply turned his snout away from the river. He looked at Perry and Stoutpoint and made a sad, bleating sound.

"We both know what that means," Stoutpoint said.

"But how can he be hungry?" said Perry. "Don't tell me he's eaten everything in that river?"

"The river's filled with as many creepy-crawlies as ever," said the horned dinosaur. "But I think Chomper's taste has evolved."

Perry sighed. "So what are we going do now?" he asked.

"It's time Chomper started doing what the theropods in the Rainy Basin do."

One of the library scrolls had discussed theropod feeding. Perry knew what they had to do. With Stoutpoint leading the way, they pushed through the swamp. Fragments of eggshells from newly hatched reptiles could be found almost anywhere. Almost as common were the remains of recently deceased reptiles, amphibians, mammals, and birds.

Almost immediately, they spotted the fresh remains of an Eryops, a giant amphibian with a flat head and body and a short tail. Chomper bolted and began to tear noisily into the dead animal with his teeth and foreclaws.

A chill rushed through Perry's body as he watched Chomper feed. This was what the Rainy Basin carnivores were like, and it was scary.

Now standing as tall as Perry, Chomper had become really good at tug-of-war. He loved playing this game of strength with his best friend.

Perry held on to a rope with all of his strength, while Chomper clamped the other end tightly in his jaws.

"You...like games...don't you, Chomper?" Perry grunted, digging his heels into the dirt in the Taylors' backyard. "But this time...you're not gonna...beat me...if I have anything...to say about it!"

While Perry pulled on the rope, he couldn't help but notice how much Chomper had changed in the year they'd been together. From tip of snout to end of tail, he was over eight feet long, which was just slightly longer than Stoutpoint. And Chomper's scaly hide rippled with muscles. Judging from the force with which the theropod pulled at the rope, the steady diet of carcasses—not to mention an infrequent blueberry dessert—had served him well. Chomper's head no longer looked too large for his body, and his legs were not overly long. The teeth lining his upper and lower jaws were strong and sharp, and the grayish and yellowish patterns on his hide were becoming more defined.

"Hey, what's all the noise?"

Perry glanced over to see Stoutpoint crossing the yard. The distraction was all that the Giganotosaurus needed. Chomper's upper lip curled slightly as his teeth neatly cut through the rope, sending Perry toppling backward.

"Oooophf!" he said.

Stoutpoint began to laugh.

"It wasn't that funny," said Perry.

"No?" asked the horned dinosaur. "Tell that to him." He pointed his nose-horn toward Chomper, who was grunting in the way Perry had come to recognize as theropod laughter.

Perry got up and dusted himself off.

Stoutpoint stopped laughing long enough to say, "You know, you really ought to think about entering the games with Chomper. Imagine! A Giganotosaurus in the Dinosaur Olympics! It would go down in the history scrolls!"

"Only if Chomper wanted to," said Perry, walking up to the theropod and patting his side. "He certainly does enjoy playing. But I'm not sure how the villagers would feel about it. Remember, Chomper hasn't been back to the village since that first time."

Chomper grunted and growled.

Perry listened and thought about what Stoutpoint had been teaching them. "Did he just say that he might like to try the games?"

"Someday," Stoutpoint said. "He may not be ready for the games, but do you think he's ready for his first fair?"

Perry hesitated. Chomper *had* come a long way. He'd left behind the frisky young theropod of a year ago and become a calm, proud, intelligent creature. He was Perry's equal in all respects.

"I don't know," Perry finally said. "I'm not sure how the other villagers would feel about it, although we know what Mr. Matthews would think."

Stoutpoint looked up at the Giganotosaurus. "What do you want to do, Chomper?" he asked.

Chomper made some sounds that Perry didn't completely understand, but he got the general idea.

"Want me to translate?" asked the Montano-ceratops.

"No need," said Perry, grasping Chomper's fore-arm and giving it a friendly tug. "Let's ask Mother if it's all right. If she says 'yes,' then we're off to the fair!"

Fifteen minutes later, Perry, Chomper, and Stoutpoint were walking through the Greenglen Village Fair.

Fruits, vegetables, and other items up for barter were displayed along the crowded main and side streets. Colorfully garbed traders shouted, and sometimes even sang, the praises of their goods. Musicians, dancers, and acrobats made their way through all the activity, sometimes scooting under the body of a towering Brachiosaurus or jumping over the spiked tail of a Kentrosaurus as they performed.

This was Chomper's first return visit to the village streets, and every sight and smell seemed brand-new. His head darted this way and that, his nose sniffed at all the scents, and his eyes followed the spectacular colors.

But the main attraction at the fair was the young Giganotosaurus himself. Some looked like they were afraid of Perry's giganotosaur friend and what he might do next. But most people smiled, impressed by how well Chomper was behaving.

"Hi, Chomper!" a village merchant shouted.

"Good afternoon, Chomper," said an Ankylosaurus. "And, Perry, give my best to your mother."

"You see," said Stoutpoint. "They like him."

"Well, most of them, anyway," said Perry, noticing Honest John Matthews scowling at them from behind his vendor's stand.

"Hello, Perry and Chomper, we see you there," sang a pair of Archaeopteryx in unison. The birds were perched on a fruit cart, their blue, red, and yellow feathers brilliant in the afternoon sun. "Welcome and please enjoy yourselves at the Greenglen Fair!"

The last words were barely out of their toothed beaks when Chomper roared. Perry wasn't certain what affected Chomper—the birds' colors, their scent, that they were just the right size to be a giganotosaur's natural prey, or if all of the fair's wondrous sights and scents were just too overwhelming for the young meat-eater.

"Chomper, no!" shouted Perry.

But it was too late. Chomper was already turning toward the birds, his tooth-lined jaws snapping furiously.

The two birds shot through the air, feathers fluttering. As the roaring Giganotosaurus came after them, his long, muscular tail crashed into a cart filled with floral arrangements and tipped it over. The birds soared off in different directions, and Chomper—not sure which to chase—turned his body abruptly. His hips and tail smashed into a half dozen carts, their proprietors running for their lives. Humans and saurians alike ran for safety, to help their friends and loved ones, and to salvage their goods. Chomper made a last effort to snag his prey, and his tail lashed to one side and cracked a fruit cart neatly in two.

Chomper was watching the birds fly off as Perry and Stoutpoint reached his side. "Come on," Perry said. "We'd better get out of here before—"

"Too late," said Stoutpoint, looking down the street.

Through a cloud of settling dust, a group of humans and saurians, with John Matthews in their lead, was approaching.

"You'd better think of something to say, quick," Stoutpoint whispered to the boy.

Grasping Chomper's thigh, Perry tried to find the right words…to apologize for what had just happened…to say that it was all an accident and nothing like it would ever happen again. But the words seemed locked inside him. After all, wasn't it all his fault for bringing Chomper into the village?

Chomper, as if realizing that he had done something wrong, lowered his head, looked toward his human friend, and let out a quiet and sad-sounding *ssqquaaawwwk*.

"You see?" Honest John shouted. He turned and looked at Perry. "You see? I told you before that bringing a wild hunter like that into the village was a bad idea. Now look at all the trouble he's caused."

Perry looked around and saw the overturned carts, the still-shaken herbivorous dinosaurs, and the worried and frightened humans.

None of the villagers needed to say anything. From the looks on their faces, it was clear that all were in agreement with Mr. Matthews. Chomper was no longer welcome in Greenglen.

CHAPTER 6

Perry disliked corrals for animals as much as he did leashes. But until the village elders could be convinced that Chomper was not a threat, the corral was the only way the young theropod could stay in Greenglen at all.

Perry was busy sawing up a beech tree trunk.

"Nice of Mr. Matthews to lend us all these tools," Perry said to Chomper and Stoutpoint, "and for nothing in trade, for once."

Chomper replied with a deep-throated laugh.

"Here's some more," Stoutpoint said, his voice muffled. The Montanoceratops was walking across the backyard with another trunk clamped in his jaws. Setting it down, he said, "Looks like you won't even have to cut this one. Seems to be just the right length."

Although he wasn't happy about the corral, Chomper was helping out in its construction—pushing logs along with his snout and biting off the ends of logs that were a bit too long.

"Your mother really did some talking to get

Chomper another chance," said Stoutpoint, rolling the log along with his snout.

Perry nodded. "If Chomper proves himself to the council elders, he might be allowed to go back into the village."

"By that time," said Stoutpoint, "he'll probably be even bigger…maybe too big for this corral."

Chomper let out a series of snarls and growls.

"He says he's really sorry again," said Stoutpoint. "He isn't sure what came over him at the fair or why he couldn't stop himself."

But Perry knew only too well. Even though he had been raised in a civilized environment, Chomper was still a theropod. As he grew, some of his natural theropod urges—like the need to hunt and devour prey—were becoming stronger. If Chomper stayed on the Taylor property, within the confines of his corral, maybe those urges could be controlled.

At least that's what Perry so desperately wanted to believe.

It was a bright afternoon, just two weeks after Perry's fifteenth birthday. Perry's mother was busy making preparations for dinner, and Stoutpoint was spending some time with his own family. It was a perfect opportunity for Perry to try out something he'd been thinking about for weeks. If what he was about to attempt failed, it was better for it to happen when no one else was watching.

As he approached the corral, Perry thought of how far he and Chomper had come in the recent months. They'd both spent a lot of time learning each other's languages, and they'd spent many hours playing games. They'd even begun practicing some of the routines the other young people and saurians were working on in the village.

Chomper looked over the wooden fence at Perry. At any time, Chomper could easily have leapt over the wall or, with a hard nudge of his head or swing of his tail, knocked it down.

Even partially obscured by the fence, the Giganotosaurus was magnificent to behold. Half-grown, he totaled an impressive twenty-five feet from snout to tail tip, and his head was more than six feet off the ground. His body rippled with muscle and steely sinew, its definition highlighted by the sunlight. And when Chomper walked and pranced about the corral, it was with the ease and grace of a mature animal.

Chomper lowered his head. His gaze went to the big leathery object Perry was carrying. The theropod made an inquisitive sound.

"You've been really good for a long time now," said Perry. "Maybe good enough to finally go back to the village. The Dinosaur Olympics are less than a month away, you know. I was thinking…maybe we should try out. I think it would help the villagers trust you again."

Chomper made another questioning sound.

"This? It's a saddle," Perry explained.

Perry had borrowed the practice saddle from Elias, who, like always, had been encouraging him to participate in the local sporting events. Chomper had never worn a saddle before, nor had Perry ever ridden a dinosaur, theropod or otherwise.

To Perry's delight, Chomper stood perfectly still, his powerful body balanced by his long tail. He let Perry set the saddle on his back above shoulder level and then buckle it securely around his massive chest.

"See, it's okay," said Perry, patting the dinosaur's side. "Now…I'm going to get onto the saddle. Don't be afraid. It's okay."

Climbing onto the saddle a few years ago would have been impossible. Now it proved to be a simple task. Chomper lowered his head slightly, and Perry jumped to grab the top of the saddle. Then the lad hoisted himself aboard.

All the while, the dinosaur remained calm.

Perry sat where Chomper's muscular neck met the shoulders, his legs hooked firmly behind the theropod's forelimbs. The S-curve of the dinosaur's neck brought Chomper's big head up almost to Perry's eye level, forcing the boy to look to either side for the best line of vision.

"So far, so good," said Perry. "Now, if this turns out like I hope it will, maybe you won't have to stay cooped up in this corral anymore."

Chomper squawked in agreement.

"Ready, Chomper?" asked Perry, looking down toward the ground. "Let's go for a ride."

Gingerly at first, and with Perry holding on to the saddle, Chomper took a few steps forward. It was indeed a new experience for the boy, and a bumpy one. Every step of Chomper's birdlike feet made the saddle—and Perry along with it—bump and bounce. Nevertheless, the more the dinosaur pranced about the corral, the more accustomed the lad became to riding him.

"N-now I want to t-try something," said Perry, his voice wavering as he bounced along. Chomper trotted along the inner border of the corral fence. "Wh-when I press my right kn-knee against your s-side, turn r-right. *Skogor*," said the boy, straining his voice to say the word in Chomper's language. "Th-think you can d-do that?"

Chomper replied with a yes, then turned sharply to the right and strode to the other side of the corral. "Now *reerack!*" said the boy from deep in his throat. "Left t-turn!"

Again, Chomper complied, turning to the left.

"G-good," said Perry. "You're a fast l-learner. Now, I wonder what the t-two of us can learn t-together?"

Perry recalled a number of maneuvers he had seen Elias and the other kids practicing in the Greenglen field. And Perry had thought up a few tricks of his own.

Chomper has come a long way since the village fair, Perry thought as he and the theropod continued their practice. Perhaps it was finally time to show everyone.

Over the next week, Perry spent much of his time in the corral working with Chomper. Now, just after breakfast, Perry was riding Chomper, with Stoutpoint walking alongside, down one of the village's back alleys.

Several human and dinosaur residents of Greenglen watched the threesome suspiciously.

"Soon they'll be cheering you," Perry said to Chomper, "once everyone sees how far you've come."

"I thought you didn't particularly like sports," said Stoutpoint.

"But Chomper seems to," said Perry. "I'll be okay."

But by the time they reached the practice field, Perry was feeling as nervous as he ever had before.

The annual Dinosaur Olympics were barely a month away. Perry knew that the young people of the village would be busy in the field, practicing with their dinosaurian mounts. Just off the field, a big tent had been set up for trading banners, clothing, and other items associated with the Olympics.

On the field itself, two ceratopsians—a spike-frilled Styracosaurus and a hook-horned Einio-saurus—were engaged in a friendly nose-to-nose game of Push and Shove, neither one able to push the other across a line that had been drawn in the dirt. A pair of Oviraptors were rolling through the dust in a wrestling contest, each trying to pin the other down with its birdlike beak. Several juvenile sauropods—a stocky Camarasaurus, a very long Diplodocus, and a smaller Dicraeosaurus—had reared up on their hind legs and, braced by their tails, were clumsily attempt-ing to stand on just one hind foot. Two stegosaurs—a small-plated Kentrosaurus and a large-plated Stegosaurus—were engaged in target practice, knock-ing over rocks by swinging their spiked tails.

Elias was the first of the group to spot Perry, Stoutpoint, and of course, Chomper. The older boy was mounted on his Gallimimus friend, Sleekneck, who wore an unadorned practice saddle.

"Perry Taylor!" shouted Elias, getting the attention of every human and saurian on the field. "Don't tell me you finally took my advice?"

"Well…," started Perry nervously, pressing his knees closer against Chomper's sides, his signal to the Giganotosaurus to stop. "We…I guess we've been practicing, too."

"Then come on and join the fun!" Elias exclaimed, waving to Perry.

Perry gulped. That old feeling was back in full strength. Perry felt as if he would rather be anywhere else but at the edge of that field.

"You sure it's all right?" Perry asked Elias.

The older lad nodded, smiling.

Truly, Chomper stood out compared to the saurians on the field. Most of the other dinosaurs were non-aggressive plant-eaters. Except for Sleekneck and the two Oviraptors, Chomper was the only theropod. Among those, only the Giganotosaurus actually ate meat. The Gallimimus and the two bird-beaked dinosaurs subsisted quite nicely on fish eggs and small bugs. Yet from their sudden uneasiness, these other theropods must have sensed that they could easily become the giganotosaur's dinner.

Perry took a deep breath of the warm afternoon air. "Okay, Chomper," he said, nudging him with his knees, "let's show them what we can do."

Perry and Chomper moved to the middle of the practice field. The three sauropods swished their tails in warning, and the ceratopsians lowered their heads defensively, displaying their great, spiny frills. The two stegosaurs gently swung their spiked tails.

"Steady, Chomper," Perry told him, his legs firmly pressing against the giganotosaur's body. "They're just acting according to their instincts. No one's going to harm you."

"If he causes any trouble this time," yelled the Kentrosaurus, "our tails and horns are ready."

"Don't worry," Elias said. "Chomper seems to have become quite civilized during his stay with the

Taylors. Let's give him and Perry a chance. Are you willing?"

Chomper looked at Sleekneck, the largest of the ostrichlike dinosaurs. Even at his adult size, the Gallimimus was about a third smaller, though much more graceful, than Chomper. As the two theropods made eye contact, Chomper greeted Sleekneck with a friendly *"Skkkrawwwk!"* Sleekneck responded with his own higher-pitched *"Skeeeeeek!"*

"You see," said Elias happily, "Chomper and Sleekneck are friends already."

"All right," shouted a teenage girl mounted on the Dicraeosaurus, "we'll give Chomper his chance."

"Well, then," said Elias, "maybe we should start with something easy. How about a simple trot across the field?"

The others moved aside, and Perry rode Chomper from one end of the field to the other. When they halted, Chomper reared back against his tail, lifting Perry higher to wave back at Elias and Stoutpoint.

"I guess you really have been practicing," Elias complimented them. "Maybe we should move on to something harder. Can you try it faster this time?"

"No problem," said Stoutpoint with a clack of his beaked mouth.

Perry nudged Chomper with his knees again, and the theropod moved forward…faster this time, building up speed and momentum. The teenager and the Giganotosaurus crossed the field one time after another, with grace, speed, and expertise.

It was on the ninth trip that something caught Perry's and Chomper's attention—a group of men and women, a half dozen in all, were carrying big, open barrels onto the practice field. Even at this distance, Perry could identify the barrels' contents: fish eggs...nuts...cycad fronds...vegetables...fruits of all kinds, including blueberries. It was a mid-afternoon snack for these training dinosaurs. The humans set the barrels atop a raised platform only yards away from the tent.

Feeling the mighty body beneath him starting to turn, Perry yelled, "Wait! Chomper!" But the giganotosaur bounded for the food barrels.

No one else on the field moved as the Giganotosaurus plowed forward and stopped at a barrel filled with fish eggs.

Perry slipped from the saddle and grabbed his friend. Though he knew it was impossible, he tried with all his might to push Chomper away. Moments later, Stoutpoint and Elias were at his side attempting to help. But not even their combined strength was enough to move the hungry Giganotosaurus.

"No!" shouted Perry. "They'll tell us when it's lunchtime!"

Chomper's big head smashed down onto the first barrel, splintering the wood and spilling its contents onto the ground. Chomper greedily devoured the first batch of eggs. What Chomper didn't eat, his feet trampled or his tail smashed.

"That's for all the dinosaurs," Perry continued, "not just you!"

But Chomper was already attacking the second barrel of eggs. When he had finally gorged himself, egg yolk and shell bits stuck to his scales and teeth and snout, he switched his attention to dessert. Reaching for the third barrel, he upset the remaining barrels...which rolled off the platform and collided with the tent.

"Chomper!" shouted Perry.

The occupants of the tent poured out, some of them clutching their products and yelling in anger and frustration.

While Chomper feasted on blueberries, the other dinosaurs opened their mouths in a resounding caco-phony of snarls, shrieks, and roars. The ceratopsians on the field thumped their forefeet against the ground, the sauropods stood up on their hind legs, and the stegosaurs swung their tails furiously. The smaller theropods stepped back so suddenly, they nearly threw their riders.

Chomper, however, paid no heed to either saurian or human. His attention was focused solely on the dark blue dessert. Finally satiated, the Giganotosaurus looked down at Perry, an innocent look on his face.

"Well," said Stoutpoint jovially, trying to break the tense mood, "at least Chomper won't have to worry about lunch today."

But no one was laughing. The athletes were still trying to calm their dinosaur mounts down. The artisans were scampering about, some of them trying to restore the tent. And Elias was glowering at Perry.

In the distance, Perry heard more voices of humans and dinosaurs. Villagers were responding to all the racket. Prominent among the approaching group, a frown on his weather-lined face, was John Matthews.

"Well, my friend, what next?" asked Stoutpoint.

Perry looked at Chomper. The theropod cocked his head from one side to the other. The pieces of blueberry still clinging to his teeth were, a moment later, wiped clean by a swipe of his tongue. Perry knew that there would be no way for Chomper to squirm out of this situation. There would be no third chance given by the council elders. Chomper had, despite his best intentions and Perry's best efforts, become a problem that had finally gotten out of control.

A weird sound issued from the theropod's mouth, telling the boy that he'd suddenly realized what he'd done.

"I know," said Perry. "We've got to do something."

Although Chomper had caused all the commotion, it was Perry who'd decided to bring Chomper to town for a second time. They would have to solve the problem together.

CHAPTER 7

At dusk several days later, Perry left the village grocery carrying the heavy sack of grains and other food supplies his mother had sent him to fetch. Heavier than this burden, however, was the weight on his mind and spirit since that day at the practice field.

No decision had yet been made concerning Chomper's fate.

"And what did your mother say?" asked Stoutpoint as the two of them walked down the main street.

"That Chomper's my responsibility and mine alone," the boy replied. "And that Chomper and I must decide what to do."

"But she must have given you some advice," said the Montanoceratops.

"She said I should think about the sick and homeless creatures I tended to over the years."

"And...?" asked Stoutpoint.

"That's all she said."

The ceratopsian nodded. "Well, you know what

you did when those animals got better."

"Yeah, I know," Perry said, feeling a rush of sadness. "I let them go."

"So…?"

"So, Chomper's not like them," argued Perry. "Not really. Not like the frogs, that little turtle, that baby Diplocaulus I rescued when I was just a kid. Chomper's a dinosaur. He thinks. He feels. He's a friend. You should understand that."

"And what does Chomper think?"

"We've discussed it. He likes living with me. But he wants to do what's best for us—for Mom, me, you, and Greenglen."

Stoutpoint nodded. "It's a hard decision to make, Perry. But whatever it is, you're going to have to make it soon. I doubt the villagers are going to wait for another incident to happen."

Perry was certain of that. As he and his ceratopsian friend walked down the street in the direction of the Taylor home, many people and saurians were in the street. However, no one was smiling, at least not at Perry; nor did the lad receive any of the usual friendly greetings.

Honest John was standing behind his vendor's stall. Mr. Matthews, Perry heard, had just returned from some mysterious visit to Waterfall City on behalf of the village council. Now his usual scowl had been replaced by a smug smile.

"You've come just in time," Mr. Matthews said as

Perry and Stoutpoint passed his stand. The merchant turned to look down the main street.

"There!" said Mr. Matthews. "Now we'll see what happens to your meat-eater!" He started to laugh.

Even from this far away, Perry could make them out—a group of large dinosaurs, possibly half a dozen, all heading for Greenglen.

"Your eyes are keener than mine," Perry told Stoutpoint. "Who is it?"

"They're still far away," answered the ceratopsian. "But it looks to me like a Pachycephalosaurus…maybe a Lambeosaurus and…oh, no!"

"What is it?" asked Perry. "What do you see?"

"I think," Stoutpoint began, his voice somber, "I think I know what Honest John was doing in Waterfall City."

It was indeed an impressive sight for a tiny village like Greenglen. Perry and Stoutpoint, along with the other residents, watched as the colorful saurian entourage walked down the main street.

Five herbivorous dinosaurs—a Pachycephalosaurus, a Lambeosaurus, a Muttaburrasaurus, an Edmontosaurus, and a Rhabdodon, all outfitted in their finest attire—were leading the way for the biggest, stockiest, and oldest Triceratops Perry had ever seen.

The horned dinosaur was immediately recognizable. Not by the red and gold garments draped across his back and head, nor by the golden trilobite-shaped charm worn around his neck. But from the broken-off horn over his right eye.

The saurian newcomers stopped in the middle of the street. The Lambeosaurus spoke. "Residents of Greenglen," he said, "it is my great honor to present Brokehorn, son of Grayback the Wise, renowned sage of—"

"Breathe deep, seek peace," interrupted the old Triceratops in a dialect that Perry had never heard before.

The other dinosaurs in the group nodded respectfully, then stepped aside, allowing the big ceratopsian to lumber forward. He swung his horned head from side to side, his ancient eyes scanning the villagers.

Mr. Matthews stepped forward. "I trust you had a safe trip?"

"A long and tiring trip, I'm afraid," grunted the old sage. "I'm not as young as I used to be. But tell me, where is this boy you've been complaining so much about?"

Stoutpoint gently nudged Perry with his snout.

Perry felt himself pale. Here he was, a boy who had never been comfortable with making new introductions, being singled out by a legendary dinosaurian sage.

"Please, young man," said the Triceratops, "I may have a big beak, but I assure you I don't bite."

Perry inhaled and stepped forward. "It's me,"

he blurted out. "I'm…Perry Taylor."

"Indeed," Brokehorn spoke again, his tone soothing. "So you are the human whose carnivorous friend has created such problems for Greenglen."

Perry nodded.

"Come with me, then, young human," said Brokehorn. "We will discuss the situation. Just the three of us. Saurian to boy to saurian."

It was already night as Perry and Brokehorn stepped up to the corral where Chomper was penned.

"Chomper, this is Brokehorn," Perry told his theropod friend. "He's a very wise dinosaur who has come all the way from Waterfall City."

Tipping his sinewy body forward, Chomper examined the moonlit visitor. Opening his mouth only slightly, the theropod made a long series of deep-throated noises.

"He said welcome to his home and that it's nice to meet you," translated Perry, this time without hesitation. Something about Brokehorn—his voice, or maybe his words—was putting him at ease.

"No need to translate for me," said Brokehorn with a chuckle. "Spending time as I did in the Rainy Basin, I've rubbed scales and grunted with a wilder crew of theropods than you could imagine. Mr. Matthews lost an arm, but I lost a horn." With that, the massive Triceratops returned Chomper's greeting in the carnivore's own language.

"He also understands my language," said Perry.

"Indeed? Impressive. So *you* are the Chomper I've heard so much about," the horned dinosaur went on. "A Giganotosaurus. Hmmmmm...seeing the big fellow behind those wooden barriers doesn't seem right at all, does it?"

"I'm sure you heard from Mr. Matthews what Chomper did at the village fair," Perry said. "And maybe you heard about what happened on the practice field, too. But Chomper's not at all like the big meat-eaters in the Rainy Basin."

Perry reached out over the corral fence. Chomper brought his head in close, rubbing his face against the boy's hand. "Chomper doesn't mean to cause trouble. See how friendly he is?"

The theropod made a rumbling sound of agreement. Then he leaned down so that his snout gently grazed the Triceratops's horny beak.

"Friendly, yes," Brokehorn said. "But to the humans and saurians of Greenglen, unpredictable. He's different from them, with needs and urges that seem alien. Needs and urges that he naturally acts upon."

Chomper grunted in agreement.

"Mr. Matthews, the others...then they just don't understand Chomper?" asked Perry.

Brokehorn nodded. "And their ignorance leads to prejudice. As long as Chomper remains in Greenglen, he will be seen by them as a threat."

The boy knew that everything the Triceratops was saying was true. "Yes, but…"

"But?"

"Chomper's my friend," said Perry, feeling his throat grow tight. "He's almost like a brother. Just like Stoutpoint."

"Friends…brothers…those we love," said Brokehorn. "What do we do for those we truly care about, Perry?"

"We…," said Perry. "We do what's best for them."

"Indeed," said the sage. "And what would you say is best for Chomper?"

"I'm…not really sure."

"I once knew a plesiosaur who loved the lake in which she lived," said the ceratopsian. "She loved the temperature of the water, the ichthyosaurs who shared the lake with her, even the land around the lake.

"But there came a day when she outgrew her lake. She was taking up space that her fishlike friends needed to thrive, and she needed more space to live comfortably herself.

"And so she swam down a connecting river to find a bigger lake, one in which she could survive and where she would not pose a threat to her friends."

Brokehorn looked up at Chomper again and said something that Perry did not understand but that had a soothing effect on the theropod. Then, turning his massive body, the Triceratops began to walk away.

"Wait!" exclaimed Perry. "You haven't told me what to do about Chomper."

"You don't need an old saurian like me to tell you what to do," said Brokehorn. "Remember the Code of Dinotopia. Then look to your own mind, your own heart…and into the spirit of your friend. All will be made clear to you…"

As the old Triceratops lumbered back toward the main street, Perry looked back at Chomper. He patted the theropod's face and pressed his own face against the cool, scaly hide of his snout.

"Don't worry," Perry told Chomper, "we're friends forever. I'll never let you down."

Chomper pressed his own face closer against Perry's, and something between a growl and a wail issued from the dinosaur's mouth.

"The Code?" Perry replied. He remembered something he had memorized years ago, one of the many things written on a scroll entitled "The Code of Dinotopia." Perry looked up at his theropod friend and quoted, "Others first, self last."

At last, Perry Taylor knew what he had to do.

CHAPTER 8

The hot sun shone from a clear blue sky.

Chomper told Perry and Stoutpoint that he was anxious to get started. He stood just outside the corral, wagging his tail impatiently. The theropod dinosaur growled at the fence that had once confined him.

"I don't blame you, big guy," said the Montanoceratops.

"No more fences and no more trouble," Perry said. "Chomper's going home."

"Just be careful," Agnes Taylor said.

She helped Perry and Stoutpoint finish packing supplies into a pair of cloth-covered bundles. They were taking blankets, various kinds of food, some cooking pots, eating utensils, and a couple changes of clothes.

"Remember, the Rainy Basin can be a dangerous place," Perry's mother added. "Don't do anything reckless."

"I'll be careful," Perry replied.

The boy grabbed the first bundle, hoisted it onto Stoutpoint's back, and tied it firmly to the horned dinosaur's body. The other bundle he kept himself, flinging it over his shoulder. Perry stretched his arms, feeling the warmth of the sun. Somehow, he felt different today, more grown-up.

Unlike Perry, the Montanoceratops was not anxious to start the trip. "You know," he said, "I never dreamed I'd ever be going to the Rainy Basin, and I'm not looking forward to it now. But if we must go, well...the sooner we go, the sooner we can come back."

"Well...good-bye, Mom," the teenager said, kissing his mother's cheek.

"Breathe deep, seek peace," his mother replied. "And good luck."

The three friends—one human, the others dinosaurian—set out toward the north.

Thick rain clouds hung over the raised drawbridge.

Working together—Perry pulling, and Chomper and Stoutpoint pushing—the three friends managed to turn the ancient wheels that worked the bonelike bridge. Slowly, the mechanisms brought the bridge down to a horizontal position.

"So that's the famous Rainy Basin," said Stoutpoint as he, Perry, and Chomper walked cautiously across the bridge. "Or should I say *infamous?*"

Just then, the rain began to fall—not hard, but enough to be an annoyance.

Stoutpoint moaned. But the rain bothered neither Perry nor Chomper.

With Perry leading, the three friends traversed the bridge and stepped onto a wet trail. The forest was a tangle of thick vegetation that grew all around them. If it weren't for Chomper, Perry would have been content simply to stop and note the names of every plant and tree.

Chomper swung his head this way and that, taking in all the new sounds and smells. Every so often, a group of tiny mammals—rats and squirrel-like creatures—darted through the underbrush.

Perry, like Chomper, also looked around, his eyes catching every movement, his ears alert to every sound.

"Hmmmm," commented Stoutpoint. "It seems that our meat-eating friend is already feeling at home, but this is certainly no place for a peaceful ceratopsian."

Perry had to agree. These woods were alive with weird sounds and even weirder smells that only hinted as to what might be waiting to spring out and attack travelers.

Chomper, however, continued to appear unaffected by the foreboding surroundings.

"It's strange, but he almost seems to know the

place," said Perry, "even though he's never been here before."

"Instinct?" said Stoutpoint. "Or maybe some basic memories—like memories of home—are passed on from generation to generation. Who can say?"

"What's important is how Chomper feels about this place," said Perry, turning to his theropod friend. "So, what do you think? Could you be happy here?"

"*Graaawwwwwk!*" the theropod replied, lowering his head closer to the ground.

"You'll get no argument from him," said the ceratopsian. "But even if Chomper likes it here, we still don't know how he'll take to living with others of his kind. Which brings up an important point. Just how are we supposed to find Chomper's kin in this wilderness?"

"We might not have to," observed Perry, looking toward the theropod.

Still walking through the wet underbrush, the Giganotosaurus lowered his head almost to the ground. The skin around his nostrils twitched as he sniffed the earth loudly, then he made a vocal sound that rose in pitch.

"You see!" said Perry excitedly. "He's doing the job for us."

"I guess it takes a Giganotosaurus to know a Giganotosaurus," mumbled Stoutpoint.

"All right, Chomper," said Perry, "Now you're leading the way."

Letting out an excited roar, the theropod stalked ahead, trampling foliage and leaving his giant tracks in the mud. Soon the three were making their way along one of the many crude trails that snaked and wound through the Rainy Basin.

"At least the local sights are interesting," said Stoutpoint, nodding toward a shattered meteorite.

"And there's a rock that looks like a pyramid," said Perry.

With Chomper clearing the way, the three friends trekked deeper into the Rainy Basin. Less than an hour later, an ominous-sounding growl rumbled from somewhere up ahead. There were other sounds, too. Heavy, pounding sounds that got louder, as if whatever was making them was coming their way.

The three friends stopped. Chomper snarled curiously and sniffed the air. His long legs assumed a defensive stance, his tail swishing high off the ground.

"Could be who we came looking for," said Stoutpoint in a soft voice. "Or maybe something else. But I'm not sure. I've never heard an adult Giganotosaurus before."

"One thing's for sure," said Perry, pointing toward the mud. Several sets of large, three-toed footprints were filling up with rainwater. "We're in theropod country."

"Quick!" whispered Stoutpoint. He pointed toward a tall growth of bushes with his snout.

Perry and Stoutpoint moved toward the bushes,

but Chomper didn't budge. Perry rushed back and pulled at the theropod's scaly leg. "Come on!" said Perry. "We don't know what species those are. They could be your kind…or something else. Better to be safe than sorry."

Chomper snorted in agreement.

Seconds later, the three of them were huddled behind the dense entanglement of forest growth.

Their wait was not long. About a hundred feet from where Perry and his companions were hiding, the foliage parted. Three magnificent creatures stepped into view. Their huge bodies—any one of which dwarfed the three figures behind the bushes—glistened as raindrops rolled off their scales.

The three towering dinosaurs looked around, sniffing. Perry could see that they were all meat-eaters. Each stood tall on muscular hind legs and possessed much smaller, two-fingered hands. The largest one must have been forty feet long. Tyrannosaurus! thought Perry as the three king theropods continued to look around.

The faces of the three tyrannosaurs were expressionless, but the dinosaurs were clearly searching for something.

"They smell us," whispered Stoutpoint.

A quiet rumble issued from Chomper's throat.

"Shhhhh," said Stoutpoint, nudging the giganotosaur with his wet nose-horn.

Chomper seemed to be curious rather than afraid.

Even though these three meat-eaters were not of the same kind as Chomper, the young Giganotosaurus felt a kinship with them. Perhaps he was recognizing these dinosaurs as distant cousins to his own species.

In silence, they continued to wait.

At last, the largest Tyrannosaurus of the group addressed the others with a series of vocal noises. The other two responded.

"They say they smell a Giganotosaurus nearby," said Stoutpoint, just loudly enough for Perry and Chomper to hear. "It seems they can't tell the scent of a young one from an adult, which is lucky for us. Giganotosaurs seem to be the only other theropod those big bullies don't like to tangle with."

After what seemed like forever, the three carnivorous giants turned, their scaly bulks quickly disappearing into the misty foliage of the Rainy Basin.

CHAPTER 9

Chomper continued leading his two friends down the trail.

By now they had ventured quite deep into the Rainy Basin. Small reptiles and shrewlike mammals jabbered back and forth and darted through the underbrush. The roars of distant theropods were carried along by the late afternoon breeze.

They stopped in a clearing ringed by tall trees. The rain was finally subsiding, and sunlight was starting to light the area.

"I don't think we're going to find a cheerier place for lunch than this," said Perry, looking around.

"No argument from me," said Stoutpoint. "We can relax for a while, too."

Perry set down his bundle and spread its contents over the ground. There were some large almonds, a healthful variety of vegetables, and several ripe honeydew melons, all from the Taylor garden.

Chomper sniffed at the food and made a sound of disappointment.

"Sorry, Chomper. I don't think Mother packed any giant worms or centipedes," said Perry.

"How thoughtless of her," remarked the ceratopsian.

"Actually, how thought*ful*," Perry corrected him. "Chomper is going back to his natural habitat. It's important that he learns to get his own food."

"*Grraawwwk!*" said Chomper, nodding.

"Good," said Perry. "Just like you did back in the swamp."

Chomper wagged his head as he talked to Perry.

Perry raised an eyebrow. "I got only half of that."

"He'd like you to go with him," translated Stoutpoint.

"Not this time, my friend," said Perry.

Chomper nodded, then stalked off into the brush.

Nevertheless, Perry had to know for certain that Chomper was not going to go hungry this afternoon. Moving as stealthily as he could, he rushed across the clearing after the giganotosaur. Peering through the brush, the boy watched as Chomper sniffed the air. Finally, he spotted something. His head darted from left to right.

Even at this distance, Perry could hear something moving through the brush. The boy turned his head from side to side as Chomper had done, but he was too far away to identify the animal. Suddenly, Chomper darted forward and snapped his mighty jaws shut.

There was a quick *shriek!*, and then silence.

Stoutpoint had spread out one of the blankets Mrs. Taylor had packed with the food. "Lunch is served," said the horned dinosaur as Perry walked back. Perry and the Montanoceratops proceeded to enjoy what was most likely the Rainy Basin's first picnic. Perry cut some of the fruits and vegetables in half to share them with his ceratopsian friend.

When Chomper finally returned, his stomach was no longer rumbling.

"Well," said Perry to Stoutpoint, "there's just one thing left for us to do."

Finishing off a honeydew melon, Stoutpoint asked, "Then we can go back to *our* home?"

Perry nodded.

"But we still don't know where the Giganotosaurus clan is," said the ceratopsian. "The Rainy Basin is a big place. So far the only Giganotosaurus we've seen around here is Chomper."

"Who knows?" the boy replied. "Maybe the Giganotosaurus clan already knows we're here."

Stoutpoint shuddered. "I'm not so sure I like that idea," he said.

"Here," offered Perry, taking a jar from Stoutpoint, "it's easier for someone with hands." Twisting off the cap, Perry revealed a jarful of dark blue fruit.

Chomper didn't have to see inside the jar to know what it contained. A quick slam of his lower jaw demolished the jar, spilling the blueberries onto the ground. Then he ate his fill.

"Hey, leave some for the rest of us!" said Stout-point.

"Don't worry," said Perry. "Mom packed another jar."

No sooner had Perry said those words when he heard loud *thump*ing sounds, like those that had preceded the entrance of the tyrannosaurs. As the sounds got louder, the ground began to vibrate.

Chomper, some of the blueberries still clamped between his jaws, snapped to attention as he sensed something huge approaching through the trees. But by now it was clear that there were more than just one something. Possibly ten or more...

Their enormous bodies soon filled most of the space in the clearing. Perry and Stoutpoint backed off to keep out of their way. There were a dozen of them in all, six males and six females, the females generally larger. Each of the huge theropods looked very much like Chomper—only bigger, more massive, older. Their teeth, shining brilliantly in the sunlight, were longer and sharper than Chomper's. Their coloring was basically the same as Chomper's, too, differing only in their yellow markings.

"I don't think we have to look any farther for the Giganotosaurus clan," said Stoutpoint under his breath.

But the giganotosaurs hardly seemed to notice Perry or the horned dinosaur. Rather, they studied with keen interest the third newcomer, for he was the one of their species.

The biggest member of the group, a male, must have been at least forty-five feet long, larger than the Tyrannosaurus Perry had just seen. The Giganotosaurus took a few steps forward, leaving the other giganotosaurs waiting behind him. His heavy feet flattened the carpet of ferns.

Perry felt as he usually did when he met someone new. This time, however, that feeling was not so severe, even though he was being confronted by a creature that could devour him in a single gulp. Struggling to recall a few theropod words, he tried to introduce himself.

The lead Giganotosaurus watched him coldly.

But the words, simple for theropods to pronounce, did not come out the way Perry had planned. "Hi," he finally said in his own language, not knowing if the huge theropod would understand him. "My name is Perry Taylor. These are my friends Stoutpoint...and Chomper."

"Chommmm-ppppperrrrr..." The dinosaur's voice was incredibly deep and grating, yet the word was unmistakable. The giant did understand! Perry thought.

The dark eyes of that Giganotosaurus focused upon Chomper, who was scarcely more than half his size. It was clear from his dignified bearing that he was the leader of his clan. He leaned over and sniffed

Chomper, rubbing his snout along the young dinosaur's neck.

Then, to Perry's amazement, the lead Giganotosaurus raised one taloned foot, stomped it hard on the ground, and squished his three toes into the mud from side to side. He squinted his eyes and hissed through clenched teeth.

Chomper, watching the leader, relaxed his bite on the blueberries still in his mouth and gulped them down.

Again the lead Giganotosaurus stomped and turned his foot.

Chomper, watching the leader, licked his chops.

A long silence followed as the Giganotosaurus leader glared at Chomper. Then he bellowed a near-deafening roar of anger and disdain. The others in his group grumbled and shook their heads.

"They don't want him?" Perry asked Stoutpoint incredulously.

"That's what it sounds like to me," answered the ceratopsian.

Chomper squawked sadly.

By now, the largest of the giganotosaurs was leading the others back into the woods, leaving behind the one who had journeyed so far to join them.

CHAPTER 10

Perry, Stoutpoint, and Chomper gazed at one another in astonishment.

"They flat-out rejected him," said Stoutpoint in amazement.

Chomper yelped his disappointment.

Perry thought for a moment. "Did you see what that biggest one was doing with his foot?" asked the boy. "Maybe that was some kind of signal or sign."

Chomper looked down and raised his foot.

"So what now?" Stoutpoint asked. "We can't take Chomper back to Greenglen, but we can't leave him here, either."

Perry was trying to think fast. "There may be something," said Perry. "Maybe…"

"What?" asked Stoutpoint. "I hope you're not going to suggest that you and I stay here with Chomper."

"I'd never ask you to do that," said Perry. "But if that's what it takes, yes, I'd stay here with him."

Chomper nuzzled Perry gratefully.

"Only I think there's still another way," the lad continued.

Stoutpoint looked puzzled.

"I don't have the right kind of throat for it," said Perry, "but you speak theropod pretty well."

"Enough to get by," said Stoutpoint.

"And that's enough for what we gotta do. Come on!"

Perry hastily gathered the items they had brought with them and bundled them up again.

"What do you have in mind?" asked Stoutpoint.

"We're going after them," said the boy.

"What?"

"Come on, we're wasting time," Perry said, tying a bundle of supplies onto the ceratopsian's back. "Those theropods can cover a lot of ground, even when they're just walking."

"Ohhhhh," Stoutpoint moaned.

Together, they started forward in quick pursuit.

Catching up with the Giganotosaurus group was not as difficult as Perry had feared. The huge dinosaurs left behind a recognizable trail of three-toed footprints and trampled vegetation. The sounds of broken branches combined with the occasional snarl or roar made it obvious where the theropods were.

Perry expected to see the gray and yellow backsides of the giganotosaurs at any moment through the foliage up ahead. And he wondered what he'd say to get their attention.

But there was no need to wonder. Perry and his friends found the giant theropods up ahead—already waiting for them.

The lead Giganotosaurus circled them deliberately. In the theropod tongue, he declared that he knew they were trying to follow him. Nevertheless, they were still not wanted. He leaned forward, bringing his grayish face just inches away from the outlanders.

Perry winced at the fetid odor of his breath.

"Grrrraaarrrrhhh!" The giganotosaur leader snarled directly into Perry's face.

In all his life, Perry had never known such fear. He was just a boy of fifteen summers. He had never done anything that compared to staring into the face of one of the deadliest predators Dinotopia had ever known. At any time, this colossus of teeth and muscle could simply open those wide, cavelike jaws and do to him what had been done to Honest John—or worse.

His knees began to wobble, and his cheeks quivered. But Perry could not reveal his fear. If Chomper were to have any chance in this realm where he truly belonged, Perry had to demonstrate his good intentions. It was his desire to do the best for Chomper, Perry thought that was saving his own life.

The theropod leader roared again.

"I think," Stoutpoint said, not sounding confident, "I think he just asked what you want."

"I know," said Perry, never looking away from the huge giganotosaur looming over him. "Why did you do that?" he asked the huge creature. "Why did you reject him? He's one of you. He belongs here."

The creature's reply came in a series of growls and snarls. As he spoke, the giant turned his massive head toward the other eleven giganotosaurs, after which they growled in agreement.

Chomper lowered his head in respect.

"So that's the story," said Stoutpoint. "Chomper cannot be one of them because he's been somehow contaminated. He doesn't know the clan's manners and greetings. He is soft and undisciplined. Worst of all, he eats the food of the herbivores. In doing so, he is not worthy of the Giganotosaurus clan."

Perry was astonished. Imagine being rejected by one's own kind, maybe even one's own family, simply for eating blueberries!

"Don't you understand?" Perry said loudly. "Chomper needs you. He belongs with you. He can't live anyplace else but here! Don't you have any loyalty for your own kind?"

The Giganotosaurus leader listened but did not answer.

Stoutpoint and Chomper stepped up next to Perry, one on either side of him.

"The human youth speaks the truth," argued Stoutpoint, his horned face looking up at the huge meat-eater. "It would honor your clan to reclaim a lost hatchling."

Once more, the lead Giganotosaurus glared at Chomper. The younger dinosaur raised his foot and brought it down into the mud, squishing it about as the bigger theropod had done earlier.

Cocking his head, the giganotosaur leader grumbled something, then nodded toward the bundle on Stoutpoint's back.

"He acknowledges the return greeting but is still bothered by the food," Stoutpoint translated. "He said the herbivores' ways will have made him weak."

"Chomper eats meat, just like you do," Perry said emphatically to the Giganotosaurus leader.

The giant leader did not respond.

Then Perry remembered something, but would it have any meaning in the wilds of the Rainy Basin?

"'Survival of all or none,'" Perry quoted from the Code of Dinotopia. "'One raindrop raises the sea.' Someday your life may depend on this young member of your clan."

The other giganotosaurs were mumbling now. Their leader walked back toward them. Huddling together, the giants proceeded to discuss the matter among themselves.

"What do you think?" whispered Perry.

"We'll know soon enough," observed Stoutpoint.

The discussion seemed to go on forever. Finally, the giganotosaurs returned to their original places.

Again their leader addressed the young human. There were too many words that Perry had never heard before, and so he looked to his horn-headed friend for a translation. He knew it was only a trick of the sunlight, but Stoutpoint's face seemed to pale.

"He said," the ceratopsian began, "that Chomper might stay with the clan—"

"That's great!" exclaimed Perry, interrupting his friend.

"He *might* stay," Stoutpoint went on, slowing down, "*if* he can pass certain tests of passage."

"Test of passage?" Perry said. "What's that? What kind of tests?"

"He didn't say," answered Stoutpoint. "Maybe a contest of some kind. I doubt these brutes have anything as civilized as our own Dinosaur Olympics. But he did say that the tests are not easy, and that they are very dangerous!"

Perry and Stoutpoint looked at Chomper.

The young Giganotosaurus, however, seemed less worried than they were. In fact, there seemed to be a determined spark in his eyes.

CHAPTER 11

As Perry and his friends entered the realm of the giganotosaurs, the boy's heart nearly erupted with excitement. Growing up in Greenglen, he had heard terrifying tales of this lawless domain. Now he was in the midst of it. Whatever happened would become a tale he would one day tell in Greenglen—if he managed to live through it!

There was no village for the Giganotosaurus community. Their realm was a forested place under the sky. Gigantic rocks, some of which had been eroded into bizarre shapes by time and weather, jutted up amid the trees. Between them were open spaces trampled to hard dirt. Many of the trees were missing their bark at the theropods' shoulder height, as if they had been rubbed against roughly. Here and there a branch as thick as one of Perry's legs was riddled with toothmarks. Apparently, they had been used as playthings in a contest or game, because they lay in the center of a large rectangle inscribed in the dirt.

Some of the giant dinosaurs were noisily feeding

on carcasses. Others, having fed already, were sleeping off their last meals. One group of males was engaged in a roaring bout with a much larger male, who seemed to be winning a contest for dominance.

Perry saw parents tending to their nests, their eggs, and their young. He saw that even the youngest giganotosaurs learned to hunt, directing their predatory instincts toward insects and very small prey. Individuals of about Chomper's size engaged in wrestling bouts and tests of strength, much as the young dinosaurs did in Greenglen. But these youngsters also ventured out into the woods to bring back the carcasses of recently deceased animals. The bigger and heavier adults tended to be less ambitious, often waiting for whatever food the smaller, swifter members of the clan brought back, and then claiming the first bites for themselves. Everyone, juvenile or adult, male or female, helped to care for the very old, injured, and sick.

Perhaps inspired by the courage Perry had displayed earlier, the Giganotosaurus leader had mellowed somewhat. Perry sensed the theropod's pride when he growled his introduction. He was Strongclaw, son of Strongclaw and grandson of Strongclaw, and had succeeded his father as clan leader more than a decade ago. When he had finished introducing himself, Strongclaw—or Strongclaw the Mighty, as he preferred calling himself—invited Perry and his two friends to make themselves at home and tour their community freely.

"It's a unique society," Stoutpoint commented as he, Perry, and Chomper made their way through the members of the clan.

"Yeah," said the boy. "They're not exactly civilized, but they're not savages, either. What do you think, Chomper?"

Chomper seemed more alive than ever, bobbing up and down when he met others of his own kind, rubbing against trees, and bowing submissively when he passed by an elder. One of the elders in particular, a female, seemed to pay an unusual amount of attention to him.

When their tour was over, Strongclaw led the three visitors to the widest and longest of the open areas. He made a long series of quiet explanatory noises, only some of which Perry understood.

"It seems that's where the tests are going to be held," Stoutpoint told the boy.

Chomper took a few steps forward to get a better look.

"Nothing special about it," commented Perry. "It's kind of like the practice field at Greenglen, only much, much bigger."

The Giganotosaurus leader spoke again.

"According to our host," the ceratopsian translated, "the tests are for young members of the clan to prove that they are adults. This isn't the traditional time of year for holding these tests, but the clan is making an exception for Chomper. The tests will be very soon. And if he passes them, he'll be allowed to stay here. If he fails, he'll have to return to Greenglen."

"Chomper *won't* fail," Perry insisted.

The young giganotosaur agreed with Perry.

Then Perry addressed Strongclaw. "Will Chomper be taking these tests alone?" he asked. "Or will he compete against other giganotosaurs?"

Stoutpoint translated Strongclaw's response. "He says that Chomper will undergo two tests by himself. But for the third, he'll be going up against another giganotosaur, one who's already passed his tests."

Chomper replied that he was not afraid.

Still, Perry was nervous about the competition. Chomper's opponent would be older, and would have had a lot of practice *before* passing his tests. It wasn't really fair. He tried to think of a way to even the odds just a bit.

"Well," said the boy, "since Chomper's opponent already has some advantages over him, may I ask that you bend the rules just a little, to make things more fair?"

Strongclaw cocked his head, then let out a low, quizzical growl.

"What I mean is, I would like to enter the contest, too," answered Perry boldly, "with Chomper. I'll ride him like the kids ride their own saurian companions back home."

The theropod leader thought Perry's words over, then raised his enormous head and let out a snarl of affirmation. Perry turned to Chomper and hugged him like a brother.

"We're going to enter the contest together," said the boy, "and we're going to win!" Then, to Strong-claw, he asked, "When will these tests take place?"

The Montanoceratops translated. "When the sun reaches its highest point above the Rainy Basin."

"High noon?" said Perry.

The horned dinosaur nodded. "Tomorrow."

Later that evening, Strongclaw snarled an order to a half dozen adult giganotosaurs. They, in turn, passed the word among the Giganotosaurus clan about to-morrow's special event. The surprise news spread quickly among the other dinosaurs in the group.

"If you're planning to do well tomorrow," advised Stoutpoint, "I suggest you both get a good night's sleep."

"It's not easy to sleep when you're this excited," said Perry. He took a blanket from his bundle and slipped underneath it. "Can you believe we have to compete tomorrow? You'd think the contest could wait at least a couple of days so we'd have time to practice."

Chomper, who was sitting on his haunches next to Perry, agreed.

"From what I saw back in Greenglen, you and

Chomper don't need much practice," said Stoutpoint. "That is, if he doesn't get hungry in the middle of some test."

Chomper lowered his head.

For a moment, Perry thought of the big mistake made on the Greenglen practice field that day, which, in a way, had led to the ordeal Chomper and he were about to face tomorrow.

Perry pulled his blanket up around his chin and settled down to sleep.

The next morning dawned with a few shafts of sunlight streaming to earth through breaks in the clouds and foliage.

Perry, Stoutpoint, and Chomper were all awake just after dawn, refreshed and hungry. A few young giganotosaurs, each about Chomper's age, approached and growled a friendly greeting, then said something more. "They're asking if he'd like to join them for breakfast," translated Stoutpoint.

Perry grinned at Chomper. "Just don't eat too much." He watched Chomper and the other theropods disappear into the brush. "You know, Stoutpoint," he said, "I think Chomper really belongs here."

After Chomper returned with the carcass he and his new friends had found, he and Perry went through some of the exercises they had performed back in the corral. They also rehearsed some tricks that none of the other youths at Greenglen, to Perry's knowledge, had ever performed with their dinosaurian mounts. And they tried out a few new tricks that the boy had been inventing all morning—special maneuvers that might surprise old Strongclaw himself.

All the while, the sun continued its ascent.

At noontime, the most expansive open area was already a hub of excitement. The entire village seemed to be taking places around the field to watch

It was almost noon when Strongclaw himself strutted onto the Giganotosaurus field, his tail held regally off the ground. He roared dramatically to the crowd.

"He is explaining to everybody the reason for today's events—who Chomper is and what's at stake," said Stoutpoint. "And now he's telling everyone how difficult these tests are going to be, as if they didn't already know."

Chomper growled that he was ready for anything and anxious to get started.

CHAPTER 12

The crowd of Giganotosaurus spectators roared a cheer. They were about to witness the first of Chomper's three tests—referred to in the community as Obstacle Bounding.

At the side of the field, Perry sat firmly mounted on Chomper's back. There was no saddle this time. But the blanket Perry had brought from home, draped across the young giganotosaur's back and fastened by a rope, served the same purpose.

Next to the boy and his mount stood their Montanoceratops friend.

"How do you feel?" asked Stoutpoint.

"Great," Perry said. Although any kind of public performance would, in the past, have terrified him, it was thrilling to experience the enthusiasm all around him. "You know, for the first time in my life, I think I understand how Elias and those other kids feel in the Dinosaur Olympics."

"And Chomper?"

The young theropod looked at Stoutpoint and

said, in words that Perry could understand, that he'd never felt better.

As these friends talked, a group of fully grown giganotosaurs were busily transforming the flat area into an obstacle course. Straining their muscles, the theropods rolled and pushed huge rocks, tree trunks, and bones onto the field.

Stoutpoint translated the rules of the test as Strongclaw spoke. "Chomper has to run across the field and jump over each of those obstacles. He can't touch a single one."

"Sounds easy enough," said Perry, his eyes scanning the cluttered field.

Chomper growled in agreement.

"If Chomper so much as grazes one of those obstacles," Stoutpoint continued, "touches it with his tail or a claw, he loses and the entire contest is over. There'll be no second or third chances."

"All right, then," said Perry. "Let's go show everyone what you can do."

They waited for Strongclaw to signal for them to start, and then Chomper trotted onto the field. A moment later, the Giganotosaurus leader roared for Chomper and the boy riding him to begin.

With Perry bouncing atop his shoulders and holding on with his hands and knees, Chomper quickly approached the first major obstacle—an enormous boulder. Struggling to hold on, Perry leaned as Chomper turned and twisted, just as they had done during their practice sessions. The force the boy was exerting on either side signaled the theropod how to move and where to turn to avoid the smaller stones and sticks littering the way.

"Now *kraga!*" Perry yelled the theropod word for "jump" as they reached the big boulder.

Chomper cleared the first obstacle without a single scale touching the enormous rock.

The crowd roared its approval!

Before the cheering died down, Perry and Chomper bounded over several giant logs and a white Tyrannosaurus skull. Again, no obstacles were touched.

Perry guided Chomper with growing precision, the two working as a unit. Leaping with grace over the last big rock, Chomper and Perry returned to the starting point. As Chomper slowed down, Perry relaxed and waved triumphantly, first to Stoutpoint, and then to the approving crowd.

"One down, two to go!" cheered Stoutpoint. He propped himself up on his hind legs and reached a forelimb out toward the two winners.

The next test, Strongclaw now told them, would not be so easy.

The second contest was called Boulder Pushing. The field had already been cleared of the obstacles from the previous test, leaving behind just one item—a boulder about the size of Chomper himself, though weighing a great deal more.

Once more, Strongclaw bellowed the rules for all to hear.

Stoutpoint translated. "All Chomper has to do is move that."

"Then that's what he'll have to do," said Perry, nudging his mount forward.

The crowd cheered again.

Up close, the enormous stone seemed even larger. It had required the strength of two adult giganotosaurs to roll the boulder onto the field.

For the first time since the event began, the boy wondered if Chomper had the strength to move it. But in past events, other giganotosaurs, just slightly bigger and stronger than Chomper, had somehow managed to pass this test. Perhaps what Chomper lacked in size and brute strength, Perry thought, could be made up for in cleverness and teamwork.

Perry gripped the pebbly skin of Chomper's shoulder, feeling the powerful muscles rippling underneath. "Ready?" the boy asked.

Chomper replied with a determined-sounding snort. He lowered his head and pushed his grayish snout against the boulder. He pressed forward, digging his claws in the dirt and straining every muscle in his legs.

"Push harder," said Perry. "*Gronngaa!* You can do this!"

The young dinosaur continued to press against

the colossal stone, straining, breathing heavily, and nearing exhaustion. Finally, Chomper relaxed and backed away from the boulder.

The stone had not moved at all.

The crowd loudly expressed its disappointment.

"Come on, you two!" Stoutpoint shouted through the din of the audience. "You can do it! I know you can!"

"You *can* do it!" repeated Perry with assurance. "You *will* do it!"

Chomper tried again. He pushed and shoved with all of his strength. He tried until his breathing became at last a simple gasp. Perry knew that Chomper could do no more.

The boulder hadn't moved.

A disappointed-looking Strongclaw stepped into the midst of the open area.

"No!" Perry shouted, getting Strongclaw's attention. "It's not over yet!"

Sometimes it took more than brute strength to win a contest, Perry thought. He tried to think of some bit of information, maybe something he'd learned at school or had read in a scroll at the library, that would help.

Suddenly, Perry smiled. The boy whispered into the giganotosaur's ear.

Listening to Perry's instructions, Chomper turned from the rock, as if about to walk away from it.

But Perry and Chomper were neither giving up

nor leaving the field. They were looking for something that had been on the field for the first test.

Among the obstacles was a sizable conifer log, longer than the ridgepoles in the homes of Greenglen.

"That should do," Perry told Chomper, who promptly scooped up the log in his jaws.

Perry slipped off Chomper's back. "We have to do this together," the boy said. He helped wedge the log against the curve of the boulder's underside. "Now push!" he said.

Chomper turned sideways and leaned against the log.

The spectators roared in puzzlement.

Perry ignored them. "That's it!" said Perry, straining. "Just a little…more. Yes, I can…feel it…it's starting to…"

It required all of their strength, but the conifer log, acting as a lever, was beginning to accomplish its purpose. As the two of them grunted and strained, there came a sound—the scratchy, grating sound of rock rolling against hard ground.

When Perry and Chomper finally relaxed, Perry saw the wriggly scrapes now marking the dirt. They had rolled the boulder!

"You know, Chomper," said Perry, regaining his breath, "I once heard it said that, using a long enough lever, you could move the whole world."

The spectators thundered their approval.

Strongclaw again spoke to the audience. Chomper

had won the first two tests, Perry understood him to say, and had to pass but one more to win acceptance into their clan. This third test, however, would be the most difficult and dangerous of them all.

CHAPTER 13

"Scale Wrestling?"

Perry said the words a few times, trying to figure out what the name of this third and last test could mean. The names of the previous tests had been quite obvious. But Scale Wrestling?

"Do you know what it means, Chomper?" the boy asked the Giganotosaurus standing beside him.

But Chomper did not have the answer; nor did Stoutpoint.

"We'll know soon enough," said the ceratopsian.

Strongclaw announced the final contest and explained its rules.

"Scale Wrestling," Stoutpoint explained, "seems to be a kind of wrestling where scale is pitted against scale."

Perry was puzzled. "Scale pitted against scale?"

"Any part of the body can be used in this test," the horned dinosaur went on, "as long as it has scales. Head, arms, tail, feet, shins, and so forth are all legal. But teeth and claws—and therefore any biting or scratching—are against the rules."

"But…I don't have scales," said Perry.

"Obviously. This is one test that Chomper is going to have to take alone."

"But Chomper needs my help!" the human insisted.

"Are you sure?" Stoutpoint inquired. "Maybe you're not giving Chomper enough credit."

The young Giganotosaurus agreed with Stoutpoint.

"Besides," the horned dinosaur went on, "only giganotosaurs can participate in this contest. It's too dangerous for humans."

Perry was almost afraid to ask, "And just what's so dangerous?"

"According to Strongclaw," the Montanoceratops continued, "the contender has to face Goldmark, the Scale Wrestling champion. They wrestle, scale against scale. And the one who walks away from the match wins."

The human youth shuddered as Stoutpoint directed his nose-horn to the Giganotosaurus now strutting onto the field.

Goldmark—noticeably older and larger than Chomper—pranced confidently about the stretch of land. He seemed to be made entirely of muscle and sinew. The champion's coloration was slightly darker than Chomper's, with a single dark-yellow spot on his brow. By the way he was moving, his self-image may have been even greater than his physical strength.

Perry frowned. "It looks like you're on your own," he said to Chomper. "But there may be other ways I can help without breaking the rules."

Chomper asked his human friend what he meant.

"Just remember the Code of Dinotopia. 'Observe, listen, and learn.' You *'listen.'* I've already done the 'learning' part for both of us."

Goldmark roared defiantly. He seemed totally confident as he and Chomper faced off in the center of the playing field.

"Remember," said Perry, standing a safe distance away. "Breathe deep and *'listen.'*"

For almost a minute, the two giganotosaurs regarded each other intently. Their eyes locked in a determined gaze. They held up their arms, claws rigid. Baring sharp teeth, Goldmark snarled a challenge.

Goldmark acted first. Lowering his large head so that its golden patch showed like some warning sign, he charged into Chomper, the force sending his smaller opponent toppling. Chomper crashed onto his side.

The spectators roared and waved their forelimbs.

"Don't worry," Perry told Chomper. "The match is just starting."

Chomper sprang back to his feet, shaking his head to regain his senses. Again the two giganotosaurs faced one another. And again Goldmark roared, although this time the roar sounded more like mocking laughter than a challenge.

"He's toying with you, Chomper," observed Perry, "trying to get under your skin. Stay focused and keep away from his tail!"

As if on cue, the older theropod turned and whacked Chomper across the face with his muscular tail. Chomper reeled from the impact. Stunned, he crashed to the ground.

This time, Goldmark didn't wait for Chomper to get up. Moving fast, he slammed his heel against the younger dinosaur's hip, keeping Chomper down. Chomper twisted his body and slipped out from under Goldmark's foot.

Again, Chomper was on his feet. But Goldmark quickly pressed his bigger and heavier body against Chomper's, their scales rubbing together. Goldmark butted his head, and then slammed his tail against the stunned Chomper. With every blow, Goldmark's superior size, weight, and fighting skills had the advantage.

"Chomper!" yelled Perry. "Get under him! Use his own strength and force against him!"

But after several minutes of intense conflict, the size, weight, and skill of the Giganotosaurus champion continued to overwhelm and pin down the challenger. Chomper's body squirmed as the padded underside of his opponent's hind foot kept him trapped against the ground.

With one foot pressing Chomper down,

Goldmark let out a roar of victory.

This is it, Perry thought. Goldmark's overconfidence and conceit would contribute to his undoing.

"Now!" shouted Perry.

Before Goldmark even knew what was happening, Chomper whipped his tail about. With a fast turn, Chomper flipped the bigger and more experienced fighter off his feet.

Goldmark fell hard.

Muscles tensing, Chomper sprang to his feet. He waited for the startled Goldmark to catch his breath and stand up again.

Without hesitation, and most likely without thinking, Goldmark charged Chomper again. This time he was met by a fast kick to his chest. Again the champion tumbled backward and crashed to the ground.

The crowd growled in amazement and approval.

To Perry's delight, the match continued in the same way. Goldmark poured all of his anger and physical might into aggressive assaults on Chomper, while Chomper turned his opponent's power against him with careful turns and thrusts of his tail, precise lunges of his snout, and expert jabs of his feet.

Goldmark was breathing heavily, his great chest heaving. He lowered his head as if to attack again.

Chomper stood his ground, the great muscles of his neck and legs tense.

Then, surprisingly, Goldmark relaxed and said

something to Chomper, most of which Perry could understand. Goldmark was tired, and he ached all over. He was surprised, but he was also embarrassed. Chomper had beaten him—how, he wasn't quite sure.

Extending a three-fingered hand, Goldmark tapped Chomper's hand, conceding victory to his opponent and acknowledging him as the new champion of the giganotosaurs. Then, saying something about a rematch, Goldmark walked off the field.

As Strongclaw declared Chomper the winner of the match, cheers erupted from all around him.

Perry rushed to Chomper's side and hugged his theropod friend. The crowd roared in approval.

Stoutpoint made his way toward Perry and the new champion. "I knew you'd win all along!" he called.

"So did I," the boy said to Chomper, proud to be sharing in his moment of glory. The young Giganotosaurus had won a home.

CHAPTER 14

That night, Chomper was welcomed into the Giganotosaurus community without pomp and with almost no celebration. There was no formal induction, testimonial speech, or initiation ritual. Chomper had won the three tests and, by doing so, had proven himself both an adult and a worthy member of the community. The main sign of recognition was a sustained community roar that lasted for several minutes.

Chomper stood beside Strongclaw. Giganotosaurs of all ages were crowding around, each trying to get a closer look at Chomper and growl a greeting.

Even Goldmark stepped up to welcome the clan's newest member. He asked Chomper if he would teach him some of the "tricks" he'd used to defeat him. Chomper agreed that he would.

"They're not much for frills around here," Perry whispered to Stoutpoint, noticing that some of the older giganotosaurs were already beginning to retire for the night.

"You're right," said Stoutpoint. "We could learn a

thing or two from these theropods. They may not use table napkins, but they're in better shape than most Greenglenners."

"If only Mr. Matthews could spend some time here," Perry mused, "and see for himself how noble these dinosaurs really are."

Stoutpoint laughed. "I doubt Honest John would recognize a noble theropod if he stared him in the face."

One group of younger giganotosaurs joined together in a cacophony of roaring that Perry interpreted to be singing. He forgot this "music" almost as quickly as he heard it. There seemed to be no melody or rhythm to keep the tunes in his mind. An extended wailing from Chomper, though, showed that he enjoyed the songs.

"They're singing about our friend," said Stoutpoint.

The night passed quickly, and Perry found himself thinking about his home, his mother, and the people and dinosaurs of Greenglen. The mission to the Rainy Basin had been successful. It was time to return home.

Perry noticed that one Giganotosaurus adult was paying close attention to Chomper. The boy recognized her as the same Giganotosaurus that had eyed Chomper the day before. Now, seeing her much closer, Perry noticed that the yellowish markings on her hide were remarkably similar in shape and number to Chomper's.

Chomper also noticed the markings. For nearly a minute, the two dinosaurs looked at one another, neither uttering a sound. Finally, the female spoke in long, drawn-out tones.

"Her name is Darkeyes," Stoutpoint interpreted as he gulped down some leaves from a nearby bush. "She says that the earthquake that rocked this land many years ago stole from her the two things most precious in her life—her mate, who perished bravely saving her life, and her only egg, which got lost in all the confusion."

Perry did not require any more translation. It was clear, from the way these two theropods were reacting to one another, that Chomper and his mother had been reunited after all those years.

"She says that she suspected the truth yesterday but wanted to be sure," the ceratopsian continued. "She has no more doubts."

Perry watched as Chomper and his mother gently rubbed faces, not unlike the way Perry and his own mother sometimes touched cheeks. What might Mr. Matthews say if he could be witness to this show of affection?

Darkeyes then spoke directly to Perry and Stoutpoint.

"She appreciates the way you raised her son," Stoutpoint translated. "And she thanks you."

Perry blushed. "Thanks, but it was nothing," he said. "When you come down to it, I'm not really sure which of us learned more, Chomper from me, or me from him."

"I'd say it was about the same," said Stoutpoint.

Darkeyes nodded. Then she moved back to join her son.

Next morning, the sky was swept clean of clouds.

"Looks like it's not gonna rain in the Rainy Basin after all," Stoutpoint said. "At least not until we're safely on our way."

Perry and Stoutpoint were standing on the outskirts of the Giganotosaurus realm, ready to leave. Chomper, Darkeyes, and Strongclaw were there, too.

Chomper was clasping something in one hand. It was whitish in color and about the size and shape of a banana.

Tipping his body forward, Chomper placed the item, which Perry could now see was a large Giganotosaurus tooth, into Perry's hand.

Strongclaw snarled and growled a long string of words.

"Strongclaw says that theropod dinosaurs shed their teeth all the time," explained Stoutpoint, "after which they grow more. This tooth was shed long ago by Chomper's father. His mother kept it as a reminder of him. Now it belongs to you. Please accept it as a token of friendship and respect. The tooth possesses great power. All in the Rainy Basin who see this tooth will know you are a friend to the giganotosaurs."

The three giganotosaurs roared a challenge to the jungle. Then Chomper growled something to his human friend.

"He wants to know if—" translated Stoutpoint.

"I know," said Perry. The boy smiled at Chomper. "Yes, I'll come back someday. It's a promise."

Perry hugged Chomper and said his good-byes swiftly.

"I guess that tooth makes you an honorary Giganotosaurus," said the horned dinosaur.

"Come on," Perry said to Stoutpoint with a smile. "Let's go home."

CHAPTER 15

Perry Taylor would never forget the adventures he and the Montanoceratops had shared with Chomper, beginning those twelve eventful years ago, when their theropod friend was a mere hatchling. Perry was no longer a shy and awkward young boy. He had developed into a man of twenty-five. He would never forget his promise to his Giganotosaurus brother.

Now Perry was standing by himself in that clearing of the Rainy Basin, dwarfed by three gigantic carnivorous dinosaurs. He had come back just as he said he would. Now he was staring into the scaly face of the biggest of the trio that had just stepped out of the woods.

And Perry was neither shy nor afraid.

Certainly, Chomper had changed over the years. His body had doubled in size and bulk. Still, despite those changes, his unique color patterns and those expressive eyes were the same as they had always been.

Perry also recognized the other two meat-eaters. The older male standing in the background was

Strongclaw, the clan leader. And the female was Dark-eyes, Chomper's mother. Of the three, only Chomper had noticeably changed.

For a moment, Perry wondered if Stoutpoint's warning had merit. Would these dinosaurs remember him and their experiences of years ago? Or had the passage of time altered, perhaps even erased, their memories?

Clearing his throat, Perry spoke a single word in theropod. *"Cchhooommppperrr."* The strain on his vocal cords was great. Then, in his own tongue, Perry went on, "Hello, old friend." He touched the theropod's snout, patting the skin like he had done so many times in the past.

Chomper spoke the young man's name as best he could in Perry's language. Then, in the theropod tongue, Chomper welcomed Perry back to the Rainy Basin.

"There's no need to tell you how much you've grown," said Perry with a smile. "But then, I've grown, too, since you last saw me."

Chomper nodded. Behind him, Strongclaw and Darkeyes rumbled approvingly.

Perry and Chomper spent almost an hour by themselves. They walked along a narrow trail, talking of the old times.

As they walked, the young man told the Giganotosaurus that his mother was in good health, that

Stoutpoint's little horns had grown as long as they probably ever would, that the sports activities were going on as always, and that Greenglen was still a prosperous and happy place.

Chomper, in turn, explained that, although he was a carnivore, he still enjoyed the occasional meatless treat.

Smiling, Perry reached into his pocket and withdrew a handful of the dinosaur's favorite dessert.

"I brought these along just in case," said Perry, holding out the clump of blueberries. "They're from Mom's garden."

Not until Chomper finished eating did Perry notice what was clutched tightly in the dinosaur's hand. It was another Giganotosaurus tooth, equal in size to the one he was already wearing. Chomper held the tooth out for Perry to take.

"One of yours?" guessed the young man, accepting the gift.

The theropod said that it was. It was the first tooth he'd ever shed here, among his own kind.

"I'll keep it always. But here," Perry said, giving back the other tooth. "I think your father's tooth belongs with you and your mother."

Chomper nudged up next to Perry and whispered something close to his ear.

For a moment, Perry again felt like that young lad he'd once been. Grinning widely, he patted the dinosaur's hip. "Sure!" he said. "I'd love to! For old times' sake!"

Looking down from his high perch, Perry could see Stoutpoint waiting at the safer end of the vertebral drawbridge.

Reacting with a start, Stoutpoint took a step backward.

"Don't worry!" Perry assured him, laughing. "Everything's fine! And I'm having a great time!"

The young man was proudly riding, this time without a saddle or blanket, on Chomper's muscular back. The last time he had taken such a ride, it was not from such a height.

"Thanks," he said, patting the dinosaur's neck. "We'll have to do this again sometime."

Perry pressed his strong legs against Chomper's body as he had done in the past, signaling the giant animal to lean forward. Perry slipped off and jumped to the ground.

Chomper asked when Perry might return again.

"How about a year from now?" answered the young man. "Let's make this an annual reunion."

The giganotosaur roared in happy approval.

"Uh, hi there, Chomper!" said Stoutpoint loudly from his end of the bridge. "Remember your old horn-headed pal?"

The Giganotosaurus answered with a loud and affirmative roar, a wave of both hands, and a nod to the Rainy Basin.

"All right," said Stoutpoint, "so I'm always welcome here, too. Well…maybe next year."

This time, saying good-bye was much easier. Perry knew that he and Chomper would be seeing much of each other in the years to come. But now it was time to return to Greenglen. For a moment, images of his village flashed through Perry's mind—Elias, whose respect and friendship Perry had earned through his accomplishments with Chomper; Honest John Matthews, who, after hearing Perry's story, had mellowed somewhat, almost becoming a friend to the Taylor household; and, of course, Perry's mother, a happier person now that most of the household duties were performed by her son.

Perry strode briskly across the bridge, looking back occasionally. He waved farewell and then began to raise the bridge. He watched the theropod turn and disappear into the Rainy Basin.

Minutes later, Perry and Stoutpoint were on their way back to Greenglen.

"I almost couldn't believe that was Chomper," said the Montanoceratops, shaking his horned head in amazement. "I mean, he's really grown up."

Perry smiled. What Stoutpoint had said was true. Chomper had indeed grown up. Yet that wasn't the only reason Perry felt so good today. Chomper was not the only one who had grown up.

ABOUT THE AUTHOR

DONALD F. GLUT has written motion picture and television scripts, comic books, and novels, including his best-selling novelization of the movie *The Empire Strikes Back*.

He is internationally known for his work with dinosaurs. He wrote the *Dinosaurs: The Encyclopedia* book series and often gives scientific lectures.

A WORD FROM DINOTOPIA® CREATOR
JAMES GURNEY

Dinotopia began as a series of large oil paintings of lost cities. One showed a city built in the heart of a waterfall. Another depicted a parade of people and dinosaurs in a Roman-style street. It occurred to me that all these cities could exist on one island. So I sketched a map, came up with a name, and began to develop the story of a father and son shipwrecked on the shores of that island. *Dinotopia,* which I wrote and illustrated, was published in 1992.

The surprise for me was how many readers embraced the vision of a land where humans lived peacefully alongside intelligent dinosaurs. Many of those readers spontaneously wrote music, performed dances, and even made tree house models out of gingerbread.

A sandbox is much more fun if you share it with others. With that in mind, I invited a few highly respected authors to join me in exploring Dinotopia. The mandate for them was to embellish the known parts of the world before heading off on their own to discover new characters and new places. Working closely with them has been a great inspiration to me. I hope you, too, will enjoy the journey.

James Gurney

Look for these other Dinotopia titles…

WINDCHASER
by Scott Ciencin

During a mutiny on a prison ship, two very different boys are tossed overboard—and stranded together on the island of Dinotopia. Raymond is the kindhearted son of the ship's surgeon. He immediately takes to this strange new world of dinosaurs and befriends a wounded Skybax named Windchaser. Hugh, on the other hand, is a sly London pickpocket who swears he'll never fit into this paradise.

While Raymond helps Windchaser improve his shaky flying, Hugh hatches a sinister plan. Soon all three are forced into a dangerous adventure that will test both their courage and their friendship.

RIVER QUEST
by John Vornholt

Magnolia and Paddlefoot are the youngest pairing of human and dinosaur ever to be made Habitat Partners. Their first mission is to discover what has made the Polongo River dry up, and then—an even more difficult task—they must restore it to its usual greatness. Otherwise, Waterfall City, which is powered by energy from the river, is doomed.

Along the way, Magnolia and Paddlefoot meet Birch, a farmer's son, and his Triceratops buddy, Rogo, who insist on joining the quest. Together, the unlikely foursome must battle the elements, and sometimes each other, as they undertake a quest that seems nearly impossible.

HATCHLING
by Midori Snyder

Janet is thrilled when she is made an apprentice at the Hatchery, the place where dinosaur eggs are cared for. But the first time she has to watch over the eggs at night, she falls asleep. When she wakes up, one of the precious dinosaur eggs has a crack in it—a crack that could prove fatal to the baby dinosaur within.

Afraid of what people will think, Janet runs away, hoping to find a place where no one knows of her mistake. Instead, she finds Kranog, a wounded hadrosaur. Kranog is trying to return to the abandoned city of her birth to lay her egg, but she can't do it without Janet's help. Now Janet will have to face her fears about both the journey ahead and herself.

LOST CITY
by Scott Ciencin

In search of adventure, thirteen-year-old Andrew convinces his friends Lian and Ned to explore the forbidden Lost City of Dinotopia. But the last thing they expect to discover is a group of meat-eating Troodons!

For centuries, this lost tribe of dinosaurs has lived secretly in the crumbling city. Now Andrew and his friends are trapped. They must talk the tribe into joining the rest of Dinotopia. Otherwise, the Troodons may try to protect their secrets by making Andrew, Ned, and Lian citizens of the Lost City…for good!

SABERTOOTH MOUNTAIN
by John Vornholt

For years, sabertooth tigers have lived in the Forbidden Mountains, apart from humans and dinosaurs alike. Now an avalanche has blocked their way to their source of food, and the sabertooths are divided over what to do. The only hope for a peaceful solution lies with Redstripe, a sabertooth leader, and Cai, a thirteen-year-old boy. This unlikely pair embarks on a treacherous journey out of the mountains. But they are only a few steps ahead of a human-hating sabertooth and his hungry followers—in a race that could change Dinotopia forever.

THUNDER FALLS
by Scott Ciencin

Steelgaze, a wise old dinosaur, has grown frustrated with his two young charges, Joseph and Fleetfeet. They turn everything into a contest! So Steelgaze sends them out together on a quest for a hidden prize. But someone has stolen the prize, and the two must track the thief across the rugged terrain of Dinotopia. Unfortunately, their constant competition makes progress nearly impossible. It's not until they help a shipwrecked girl named Teegan that they see the value of cooperating—and just in time, because now they must face the dangerous rapids of Waterfall City's Thunder Falls!

FIRESTORM
by Gene DeWeese

All of Dinotopia is in an uproar. Something is killing off *Arctium longevus,* the special plant that grants Dinotopians long life—sometimes over two hundred years! As desperate citizens set fires to keep the blight under control, Olivia and Albert, along with their dinosaur partners, Hightop and Thunderfoot, race to find a solution. But Olivia is secretly determined to claim all the glory for herself. In her hurried search for answers, what important questions is she forgetting to ask?

THE MAZE
by Peter David

Long ago, a Raptor named Odon left Dinotopia's society to live in a dangerous maze beneath the island. Despite their fears, Jason, Gwen, and a witty young saurian named Booj are determined to reach Odon. Gwen's father is suffering from a deadly disease, and Odon, once Dinotopia's wisest healer, is their last hope for a cure. Will the three friends make it through the Maze? And even if they do, how will they ever convince the mysterious hermit to help them?

RESCUE PARTY
by Mark A. Garland

Loro is a young boy who dreams of adventure. He wants to travel, while his stepsister Ria is happy keeping up with everyone in their hometown of Bonabba. The problem is that Ria and their Styracosaurus friend, Trentor, can hardly keep up with Loro.

When a deadly storm hits Bonabba, the three friends witness a hot-air balloon heading toward the Rainy Basin. Trentor is worried about his father, a Basin trail guide, and Loro wants to follow the balloon. Soon Loro's dream comes true as he and his friends embark on a mission to rescue and explore. But are they walking into danger?

SKY DANCE
by Scott Ciencin

Ever since he was small, Marc has wanted to be a tightrope walker—even though he has no sense of balance and a fear of heights. His buddy Gentle, a Parasaurolophus, dreams of being a musician—even though his notes are wildly out of tune. Through sheer determination, the two join a troupe of traveling entertainers. They learn quickly, but their newfound skills are put to the test when tragedy strikes. A Sky Galley is sent wildly out of control during a terrible storm. Only an aerialist like Marc can save the passengers. But performing isn't easy when lives are on the line!

Some Favorite
Dinotopian Expressions

"To have strong scales" = to be tough, to have thick skin

"To roll out of the nest" = to leave the island

"To crack through the shell" = to pass into adolescence

"A rolled-up scroll" = someone whose behavior is puzzling or unpredictable

"Something is boiling in the pot." = Something is about to happen.

"To look at someone from horn to tail" = to look someone up and down

"To be in the horsetails" = to be lost or overwhelmed

"To be in someone's scroll" = to be in good with someone

"Sing and it will go away." = Take your mind off your troubles.

"Jolly-head" = someone amusing

"Head-scratcher" = worry, problem

"Breathe deep, seek peace." = Take it easy, peace be with you, farewell.